# Can Macron offer Biden the Restoration of Women's Abortion Rights?

The EC Publishing LLC books may be ordered through booksellers or by contacting:

EC Publishing LLC
116 South Magnolia Ave.
Suite 3, Unit F
Ocala, FL 34471, USA
**Direct Line: +1 (352) 644-6538**
**Fax: +1 (800) 483-1813**
http://www.ecpublishingllc.com/

Ordering Information:
Quantity sales. Special discounts are available on quantity purchases by corporations, associations, and others. For details, contact the publisher at the address above.

Printed in the United States of America

# Can Macron offer Biden the Restoration of Women's Abortion Rights?

## Lamarck has returned with Jesus Christ

A book in Korean-English
translation by Kwon Sung-hee

People of France! Do you know that Lamarck was right, not Darwin! Lamarck's daughter prophesied that posterity would relieve her father's resentment.

God's justice is Lamarckism, sin is Darwinism, and the judgment will be made accordingly.

According to Darwinism, God is nothing more than a delusion or parasite in the brain, but according to Lamarckism, God is the ultimate scientific presence.

Darwinism can not explain abortion and homosexuality, but according to Lamarckism, these are typical life phenomena.

# Author **Kwon Sung-hee**

Author Kwon Sung-hee is a divorce lawyer with 35 years of legal experience. While scientifically analyzing 'the phenomenon of couples combining opposite personalities even though personality differences are the biggest reason for divorce', she came to evolutionary biology and discovered the greatest long-cherished pursuit of biology, 'The sexual reproduction mechanism and the new theory of evolution'. She then wrote her findings on this in her book titled: <The Evolution of Sex Through the Inheritance of Life Cycle and Speciation as a Result of the Use and Disuse of Organs>. (August 2021, Evolution and Humans). Nicknamed as 'Lamarck's daughter', self-proclaimed 'Jesus' lawyer' sent by John's Gospel 14 ~16, she claims to have been called to consummate Western civilization by integrating religion and science. She is living in Seoul, South Korea.

## Career

- 2022~2023: Senior Vice President of the Korean Bar Association
- 2021: Publication of <The Evolution of Sex Through the Inheritance of Life Cycle and Speciation as a Result of the Use and Disuse of Organs>
- 2015~ Present: Chairman of the Family Matters Community, Seoul Bar Association
- 2011~2012: KBS AM Plaza, 'Wednesday Family Research' Panel
- 1991: <Twenty-Four Years Old of Women > (co-author)

In Memory of Jean-Baptiste de Monet, chevalier de Lamarck,

In addition to publishing the book in the United States, I would like to especially thank Professor Denis Noble and President Emmanuel Macron. God loves the truth, and as apostles of the truth, you two have been invited to join me in the ministry of 'the Return of God, that is, the Achievement of the Scientific Nature of God and Religion', which is symbolized by the 'Second Coming of Jesus', and I am greatly honored to inform you of this.

To American women whose abortion rights have been violated, to all sexual minorities including homosexuals, lesbians, and transgenders, for feminists, and for all those in solidarity with them, including Presidents Macron, President Biden, and Pastor Lee Dong-hwan.

"I am the Alpha and the Omega," says the Lord God, "who is, and who was, and who is to come, the Almighty."
(Revelation 1:8)

God is a scientific being that evolved along with Homo Sapiens, who acquired language as a tool for thinking in the process of evolution of the genus Homo and lived by knowledge, while coping with the ignorance that constantly causes anxiety. In Lamarck's theory of evolution, God and man are twins.
(Kwon Sung-hee, PowerKorea March 2023 issue)

In a debate between the Professors Denis Noble and Richard Dawkins dated December 1, 2022, Professor Noble declared, "It has been experimentally proven that traits acquired in (somatic) cells are transferred to the germline. The Lamarckian theory of evolution has been revived. To be clear, we can say that the inheritance of use and disuse has now been clearly revealed," (Even Professor Dawkins said, "Darwin's gemule serves to look back on the current state of the body and pass on what it has learned to the next generation." He admitted that Darwin turned to Lamarckism in his later years.)
(Youtube video from the date above)

Modern theorists have recently expressed great doubt as to whether the term 'science' can any longer be used in the field of religious studies, other than appeals to evolutionary biology and genetics. If pioneers working in genetics, neuroscience, and evolutionary biology begin to explain religiosity based on the universal structure of the brain, etc. then, our dilemma will be resolved by a true general theory based on the so-called biology of belief.
(Daniel L. Pals, 'Eight Theories of Religion')

Although the modern worldview (which began with the Enlightenment in the 17th century and the emergence of modern science in the 18th century) still dominates Western culture, I am convinced that the day will soon come when the modern worldview will seem as outdated and bizarre as the Ptolemaic worldview. I am convinced that the Sacred is real.
(Marcus J. Borg, 'The Meaning of Jesus : Two Visions')

Christian language such as resurrection, ascension, and the second coming is now passing through an era of crisis. I believe that the 'underlying fundamental reality' this ancient form of narrative seeks to express is truth. However,

the method of expression is so outdated that it misleads us. Now the need for expression in a new language has become acute. But we can't rush it. In time, as always, it will emerge by itself from somewhere on the borderline between the conscious and the unconscious, where the imagination and the world, as well as myth and history, collide.
(Harvey Cox, 'When Jesus Came to Harvard')

# Prologue

At the end of February 2023, just before my term as Vice President of the Korean Bar Association ended, I published a Korean-English book of this same title, and I shouted at people. "The book in 2021 made a scientific discovery and the book this time aims to get recognition of that discovery." On February 28, I sent 28 volumes each to President Biden, President Macron, and First Lady Brigitte by DHL. I signed only one book of the 28 volumes without personal letters, but sent it to President Biden with A4 paper with 'JESUS SENT' in hand written. Of course, I am qualified to do this.

These books were mailed as follow-ups to the first mails sent to the French President and First lady, so I sent them separately again. Each offering was intended to increase the likelihood of exposure and attention of as many people as possible. After much consideration, I also decided to send it to President Biden because he is the leader of the United States, a country involved in the tragic issue of abortion for women. How big is the White House? I couldn't imagine reaching the president. It was the same in France, although I had some ideas. Then, on March 8, 2023, World Women's Day, an email came from the Elysee Palace. I never even imagined this.

Surprisingly, it was a thank-you letter for the first mail sent in early February. People disparaged it as a formal greeting, but I immediately recognized that the letter was evidence of a promise from the Christ. Jesus always said, "Keep watch," and I was able to clearly see how awake France was. At the end of March, a friend sent me a YouTube link of the debate of the century between Professor Denis Noble and Professor Richard Dawkins under the title 'The Age of the Selfish Gene is Gone'. To me, this too was a sign of the Christ's promise.

Early April, I immediately read Professor Noble's 'Music of Life'. In the book, the microscopic world of Lamarck's theory of evolution was perfectly embodied. My discovery, on the other hand, was the macro world of Lamarckian evolution, so it was a perfect fit. I wanted to go to England to meet Professor Noble. I sent an email and received a response, but I was soon disconnected. It turned out that my email was the first in line of thousands of other email. It was just a miracle. While reading Professor Noble's book, I found out that Eom Yung-ui, professor emeritus at Seoul National University School of Medicine in Korea, is close to Professor Noble. However, I couldn't just contact him blindly. This is because scientists are very busy and have high self-esteem.

In mid-June, I happened to defend the case of an urban climber, who was arrested for climbing Lotte World Tower, for just one week. I also regard this as a sign of the promise sent by the Christ. when I saw pictures of people climbing the vertical skyscraper without any safety equipment, my self-image overlapped as I heard a voice saying, "I'm proud of you for challenging the impossible!" There was a 5-day international book fair at COEX in mid-June. I didn't even look at it because I felt like I wasn't ready to go abroad yet, but at the last minute, I thought, 'International Book Fair? Where else do I find an opportunity like this?' When I arrived in a hurry, it was 2 pm. "If it is the Lord's will, please let me happen to find one publisher from America."

I left home with two copies of the book I wrote in Korean and English and a copy of monthly PowerKorea March 2023 issue. I gave them to the same publisher I'm currently working with. Two of the employees preparing for closing the booth were sexual minorities. They were amazed when I told them about their biological origins, and they said they were shocked enough to have goose bumps while they were hearing me. When they returned to the United States, they contacted me so diligently that I was a bit annoyed to be honest. The fact was that I was afraid. As a total stranger, what do I know about America?

However, these two events suddenly aroused the courage to contact Professor Eom Yong-eui. Am I not the one who should get help from one of the nation's top scientists more than anyone else? I introduced myself as such, and cordially made request for help from Professor Noble. Eom was very kind. To my surprise, he was traveling in France with Professor Noble. I thought things were working in my favor. He agreed to meet me after returning home. My prayer this year was to achieve my goal easily. As the purpose of the attempt is so great, the method to arrive the destination is to ensure that the person arrives safely, 'like a traveler returning home safely.'

I continued my study regarding the elements of the Second Coming of Jesus in the New Testament, and learned that Jesus will come before this winter. This is because Jesus said, 'This will not be in winter,' and all other external conditions for Jesus' Second Coming were fulfilled. In particular, after the arrogant intellectuals killed God, evil gained the upper hand, and as a result, the U.S. Supreme Court made an outrageous ruling, and from this point on, persecutions of abortions and of sexual minorities began to occur around the world.

Especially, I did not want this year to pass because I believed that my findings should not have a direct impact on next year's US presidential election. I personally support President Biden, who has a youthful spirit that never ages, and has ideals and good intentions that can be trusted at any time. Yet I believed that it was fair for the Republicans to take the opportunity to reflect on the implications of my findings and to face off on presidential election on policies other than Christian issues.

The way for Jesus to return was through the publication of my 3rd book, which briefly outlines the 'fulfillment of the requirements for the Second Coming of Jesus.' Otherwise, people around the world would not know that the time for Jesus' Second Coming was imminent. So I knew I had to write a book before this winter. Then, at the end of July, the news about room temperature superconductor LK99 made the world buzz. I immediately saw that it was also a sign of promise from the Christ to me. This is because my request to President Macron earlier this year to 'make my findings public so that both scientists and the ordinaries can publicly verify' was being worked on.

"Not only Korea has LK99 but also LK100. People of the world, please verify this too." I really hoped that LK99 would be successful, but 99 is the number just before completion. Since my discovery was already made two years ago, it can be said to be that. LK is the first and last letter of LAMARCK while 100 in Korean reads 'back' which means in English 'return'. In the end, it became 'LAMARCK BACK'. You can conclude that my interpretations above are unscientific. However, the Christ did not hide that He continued to support me by giving me the phrase 'the power of coincidence.' Religion inevitably has an element of mystery, which is an enigmatic feature of Sapiens behavior.

In mid-August, while I was processing disciplinary action

from the National Fire Agency in Sejong City, I received the news that Professor Eom would be returning to Korea at the end of August. Since Sejong City is a city named after King Sejong the Great, who created the Korean Alphabet, it was consistent with my discovery that Sapiens evolved by acquiring language, and I knew that Professor Eom would be helpful to me. However, I was caught up in the handling of cases in the apartment where I was living, and I was dragged along helplessly, unable to find time to write the book. After all, will Jesus return next spring?

Then, at the end of September, I celebrated my 60th birthday on Chuseok, the Korean Thanksgiving by lunar Calendar. It is the day of full moon, a day to celebrate the harvest of the year's hard work. Grace poured out from the Christ, including learning the meaning of my birthday and the meaning of my name. I realized that just as the Christ harvested the seeds sown by God, I too was reaping what the Christ had sown. I learned that the Christ, who became God, had chosen me, an unknown person from the East, as His representative in inviting women to play leading roles in history. My public ministry began last year, 40 years after my audience with the resurrected Christ, and He made me wait until I reached the age of 60 to harvest the fruit.

It reminded me of the American publisher I met at the international book fair. It has been 100 days since I met them, and the publisher deals with Christian books. It took me 100 days of warm-up to get them on the same page. When I contacted them, they were delighted, and we made it to where we are today. Their unwavering publishing policy actually gave me confidence. They proposed separating the English section of my Korean-English book and publishing it in the US. Why not? I instantly agreed. I insisted that it be done before Thanksgiving. This is because it was still possible before winter for the Second Coming that Jesus promised. They respected my wishes, and I was very grateful.

I gave this news to Professor Eom, who had been sending me brief messages from time to time. He praised me for doing a good job. Since I didn't know when or how he would provide me with decisive help, I thought I should meet him in advance and give him two of my books, so I did just that. After some time, I heard surprising news from him. He said that Professor Noble was visiting Korea, and that he would arrange for me to meet with him for about an hour. Since he is 87 years old, I had hoped that I would be able to visit England sometime this year, but on the contrary, the professor would visit Korea? I knew that the Christ loved the professor so much. The professor was born with outstanding intelligence and is one of the greatest scholars of our time who has sincerely devoted his entire life to the truth, both professionally and personally. He is passionate about Buddhism and has excellent knowledge of it.

Seeing the world's greatest scholar means the Christ letting me know that the promised time had finally arrived. That I, an unknown amateur scholar from the East, would jump to the top of the world and soon discuss the truth with a great scholar. The Christ said, "The truth is one. The truth cannot be divided into two," and He said in particular, "Professor Noble and I are the ones who bring peace to the East." As I thought about what it meant, I realized that the Christ wants peace in ongoing wars, especially wars waged by religion. I realized that when Professor Noble declared on December 1, 2022 that the Lamarckian world of peaceful coexistence had arrived, He was praising the fact that it had already been accomplished. The East meant Jerusalem.

I also knew the fact that the great scholar, not me as young, came to Korea meant that he came to pay homage to the presence of truth behind me. The Christ announced that He was willing to immediately reconcile with the scientists of the world because of the Great Scholar. Personally, I feel very fortunate that Professor Noble, a fellow Briton, is taking the lead in overthrowing Charles Darwin's world view as it was known so far. The professor said that Darwin turned to a Lamarckian in his later years. I hope that truth becomes known to the world. I met Professor Noble October 27, got his autograph on his book, and gave him two of my books.

Publishing in America usually takes 3 to 4 months, so I had to cram again to publish a book before Thanksgiving. I had to add what I had learned specifically about the Second Coming of Jesus from the end of February to the present, and I had to add crucial information about the integration of science and religion. I even had to write a prologue that wasn't in the original book. In addition, I decided to attach the findings report at the end of 2021, the letter sent to President Macron, and the interview contents published in two issues of monthly PowerKorea. The intention was to enable scientists and the general public to better understand my discoveries by reading what I wrote about them in various ways, so that they could easily participate in scientific verification.

Lamarck also paid a heavy price for discovering the truth. As he was the first to advocate the theory of evolution, he received criticism close to a curse from his contemporaries who believed in creationism, and later suffered severe ridicule and insults from his distant juniors in the scientific community. Professor Noble, President Macron, and I are parties that share Lamarck in common. In particular, in relation to Professor Noble, since it is 'expressed through religious symbols,' I especially ask him not to feel uncomfortable. If the best scientists and believers in God are like this, who can be confident that they are free from dogma? But who are we, the Sapiens species? Isn't this the species that has 'Jesus Christ, the Son of Man'? Can we see the true value of Jesus now? Can life on Earth reject light?

November 3, 2023

# Contents

# Premise

On June 24, 2022, the U.S. Federal Supreme Court broke the 49-year history of Roe v. Wade and made abortion rights dealt independently by each state. As a result, numerous abortion clinics have closed in many states and American women are experiencing a catastrophe.

Meanwhile, French President Macron, who promised solidarity with these American women who have lost abortion rights, was to pay a state visit to the U.S. on December 1, 2022. Nicknamed as the Daughter of Lamarck, Kwon Sung-hee, who also is an enthusiast of evolutionary biology and a self-claimed advocate of Jesus, claims that Macron was entrusted by God with a mission of restoring abortion rights of American women.

The claim seems huge and absurd. However, loss of abortion rights is a major crisis for American women, and since there is no clear solution to that matter, it might be a good idea to listen to her claim. She is, after all, a highly experienced divorce lawyer and Senior Vice President of the Korean Bar Association.

While dealing with divorce cases for a long time, she found it ironic that couples combine opposite personalities, even though the biggest reason for divorce was personality differences. She started researching the evolution process of human brain from the year 2016 to see if there is a scientific secret hidden behind this.

During the course, she encountered the theory of evolution. She doubted Darwin's passive view of biology that organisms are selected rather than adapted to their environment. Instead, she was attracted by Lamarck's active view of biology that organisms use their internal will to adapt. Driven by the latter's idea, she decided to explore further until she finds something more convincing.

The fruits of her passionate wandering for more than

five years were resulted in abundance. She discovered the mechanism of sexual reproduction, a long-cherished pursuit of biology. And she concluded that the biologists had adopted Darwinism unreasonably for a long time, despite the fact that since speciation is the principle of formation of male and female, and it is impossible to know speciation without knowing the evolution of sex.

She was able to prove Lamarckism was right: male and female evolve simultaneously by use and disuse of somatic cells (organs) in the order of 'pre-survival, post-reproduction'. At the end of August 2021, she compiled her findings into a book <The Evolution of Sex Through the Inheritance of Life History and Speciation as a Result of the Use and Disuse of Organs>. (In the English title of the book, 'Life Cycle' is correct rather than 'Life History', but I will not change it one by one in this book.)

However, the closing of her book was just another starting point. Because God appeared and said to her, "I have been waiting for you. I am the science." Having absorbed in the study of science for 5 years to have found 'the new biology', God ordered her to prove the scientific nature of God.

Kwon remembered the first time she read the Bible in a missionary course in college. In broad daylight, Jesus appeared in front of her and said, "The truth will set you free." She knew it was a reenactment of Jesus' Resurrection. She also remembered hearing from her heart countless times in her high school days that she is the one who consummate Western civilization. She finally came to know that she had received a call from God to seek the truth, and that by integrating religion and science, she had been given the mission to consummate Western civilization.

According to her, Jesus was a super intellectual who foresaw thousands of years. He established a universal religion through witnessing the Roman Empire, seeing the irreversible transformation of the civilization, and the need of thorough separation of church and state alongside people's comfort through religion.

By Christianity which began in this way, persecuting the aborted and the sexual minorities such as homosexuals and transgenders is but severe misunderstanding the will of Jesus. Sent as the Jesus' advocate by John 14-16, she claims to be the one who proclaims the truth through judging the sins of the world and the righteousness of God, and that Macron, the politician most worthy of Jesus' intentions, has the authority to welcome Jesus back to us forever.

She sent the documents containing this to the French

Embassy Seoul on September 30, 2022 so that President Macron would visit America with the good news. But since she has not been contacted from the Embassy, she decided to interview herself to spread the good news. (She asked a number of newspapers to interview her, but was refused.)

# It is such a huge story that I do not know what question to start with.

Do you know what Jesus said to the weeping women who followed him on his way to the hill of Golgotha to be crucified?

"Women of Jerusalem, stop crying for me. Instead, cry for yourselves and for your children, because the time is surely coming when people will say, 'How blessed are the women who couldn't bear children and the wombs that never bore and the breasts that never nursed!' And if they do this when the wood is green, what will happen when it is dry?"

Is Jesus on the side of the women who have abortions, or on the side of the Christians such as the U.S. Federal Supreme

Court Justices? Did not Jesus already foresee today 2,000 years ago? The persecutors of abortion should be ashamed and must shout to the mountain, "Fall on us!', and to the hills, Cover us up!" (Luke 23).

What do you think is the function of religion? Can a religion that believes in God persecute others for any reason? In what era do you dare to persecute people by misrepresenting some old verses of the Bible? Did not the modern democratic state built on the modern revolution declare in its law that 'all human beings are equal'? Jesus taught, "Don't judge" and he never judged or condemned himself. Now that Jesus has finally returned in the last days, let us wait and see who will be judged.

· · · ·

# Is it really possible
# to restore abortion rights?

It is possible through a paradigm shift from the current Darwinism to Lamarckism.

Darwinism identifies sex, by sex chromosomes (XX, XY). And it also identifies life as a gene cloning machine. Therefore, it does not explain the biological justification of the aborted and the sexual minorities: relationships between persons who do not give birth, or those who perceive themselves as the opposite sex of their sex chromosomes.

Lamarckism, on the other hand, views life as the result of actively adapting to the environment through internal will.

It sees that there are, of course, legitimate biological reasons for abortion and sexual minority phenomena.

Darwinists and Christians seem to be at odds with each other. But we must see that they are actually cooperating with each other. Because, scientists gave Christians a keen tool called 'gene' for persecution, and this is happening within the Darwinian paradigm.

Upon entering the main gate of the Botanical Garden of Paris in France, there is a statue of Jean-Baptiste de Lamarck, the founder of biology. There is a relief of Lamarck and his daughter on the back of the statue. At the foot is written as follows: "Posterity will admire you; It will avenge you, my Father." Now that the time has come and the posterity have appeared, the daughter's prophecy will come true.

On Parents' Day 2021, my biology studies, that took many years and never knew what would happen finally, aroused my family's concerns. At the time, the progress of my book had reached around 90% to be completed, I decided to stop there and publish it right away. The next day, May 12, I wrote on my Facebook "I will turn stupid Charles Darwin into stone dust. Just a little more patience." Exactly 5 days later, May 17, I heard the news that Darwin's Arch to the southeast of Darwin Island in the Galapagos Archipelago was collapsed in front of the tourists on that sunny day. It was the holy ground of Darwin's theory of evolution. I was calm, but people around me were clamoring that it was a sign that I would see the light of the day. (The cover design of this book symbolizes the collapsed Darwin Arch.)

Darwinism has been a dominant theory in the scientific world for a long time. How can we make a paradigm shift to Lamarckism?

We can make the paradigm shift by understanding the sexual reproduction mechanism, a long-cherished pursuit of biology, and its new speciation mechanism. Most animals, including humans, are divided into male and female, and plant flowers also have pistils and stamens. In biology, figuring out the origin of male and female, or why multicellular organisms reproduce through sex, was the last big task.

Evolution, or speciation, is the principle of the formation of male and female members of a species. So it is my impression that without first understanding sexual reproduction, it is impossible for us to know the speciation. Luckily, after understanding the evolution of sex, I found that Lamarckism was right. It was obvious that the evolution of sex and speciation were inseparably intertwined.

In the order of appearance, organisms can be divided into three: single-celled prokaryotes in which chromosomes are scattered like threads in the cytoplasm; eukaryotic single-celled organisms in which chromosomes are contained in the nucleus (referred to as 'protists' for convenience); multicellular organisms composed of numerous cells that each cell shares a nucleus containing the same chromosomes. As we will see later, descendants have elements of prokaryotes.

All organisms have life cycles for survival and reproduction. Sexual reproduction was evolved, by the descendents, protists and multicelluar organsms, when they need, through inheriting the life stories of the ancestor as combined form, but applying them as modified form to suit its own system such as the presence or absence of a nucleus or multicellularity, in the process of survival and reproduction. As it turned out, not only the life history, but also the traits of the ancestors were inherited and applied to the descendants.

In other words, protists and multicellular organisms called the life history and traits of prokaryotes as necessary and applied or modified to use. Multicellular organisms also inherited the life history and traits of protists and applied or modified them. I will never forget how amazed I was after knowing this! Organisms actively adapted to their environment, but never passively chosen or eliminated by nature!

# You said that you discovered the sexual reproduction mechanism for the first time. Can you explain it in more detail?

What is difficult in scientific discovery is 'to discover'. But once it was discovered, people would say "Was that it? I might have found it too." A typical example is the evolution of sex. People might be more curious about sexual reproduction in animals and plants. But sexual reproduction was first evolved by protists. So let us first briefly review the core principles of the sexual reproduction of protists. This makes it easier to understand the sexual reproduction of multicellular organisms later.

Prokaryotes have 'horizontal gene transfer' as their life

cycle. It is a phenomenon in which a small piece of gene called a plasmid is carried and passed on to other prokaryotes unilaterally. Some prokaryotes form 'endospores' when the environment is unfavorable, but they become active again when the environment improves. Prokaryotes reproduce by self-replication by the method of binary fission.

When the environment is unfavorable, protists clone their somatic cells to become two, and then they are mutually spliced to form strong diploids. When the environment improves, the diploid undergoes meiosis and returns to its original trophic form and reproduce by self-replication. This is called 'sexual reproduction'.

Here, 'the phenomenon of joining two somatic cells to become diploid and undergoing meiotic is analyzed as a phenomenon in which the horizontal movement of genes in prokaryotes is inherited but modified to fit the system of protists with nuclei. At this, diploids combine the properties of 'endospores' too. In other words, protists inherited with combined form of genetic horizontal movement with endospores of prokaryotes, and used them for sexual reproduction.

'Self-replication' for splicing into diploid is interpreted in biology as 'forming germ cells'. Because, it leads to the result of reproduction. Therefore, in order to facilitate mutual bonding, they are cloned by dividing them into sperm and eggs. This way, they can easily detect each other.

# 05

# What is inherited is not DNA, but life history or traits themselves. It is difficult.

Yes, because you heard it for the first time. It is simple once you know. It can be easily understood that descendants such as protists and multicellular organisms inherited the life history or traits themselves of their ancestors as needed, but modified and applied them according to whether they have a nucleus or they were unicellular or multicellular.

The 'symbiosis theory' that protists evolved as a result of preying on prokaryotes is an established theory in the biological world. Since multicellular organisms lead underwater sessile life in the early stages of evolution, it was believed that protists evolved by acquiring multicellularization factors through processes such as sedimentation or compression on the bottom of the water. Some protists tend to form colonies to cope with unfavorable conditions.

Then, it must be said that all descendants have elements of prokaryotes, and, if necessary of course, the life history or traits of prokaryotes can appear? French molecular biologist Jacques Monod said, "What works for Escherichia coli also works for elephants." I believe this is the true meaning of what I just said above.

In order for descendants to inherit the 'horizontal transfer of genes' that acquires chromosome fragments between prokaryotes, they undergo somewhat complex modifications depending on whether there is a nucleus and whether they are unicellular or multicellular. On the other hand, endospores with hardening properties and self-replicating reproduction by binary fission simply seem to be inherited for the purpose of use in traits or life history.

The hard cysts of amoeba or ciliate, the spores and seeds of plants, the fertilized eggs or eggs of wintering insects, and the eggshells of birds and dinosaurs are hard. Is it not because they inherited the hard traits of the endospores of prokaryotes in order to exploit them as needed? What about the bones and teeth of vertebrates?

What about the immune system? Could it be that the principle of immune antibody formation in human somatic cells is inherited from prokaryotic CRISPR? Do not all species have their own immune systems?

The self-replication method, which is the original reproduction method of prokaryotes, is also inherited as it is, and descendants inherit with or without nuclei, single-celled, or multicellular, and replicate each usual trophic type.

In other words, what is inherited is a trait or a life history, not the DNA or gene. If DNA replication is so important, why not partial replication? And if asexual reproduction is somatic cloning, why not sexual reproduction? The germ cells of protists are formed by division of somatic cells. Shouldn't the germ cells of multicellular organisms, which are essentially protists, also naturally be formed by the division of somatic cells either mitosis or meosis?

# 06

# What does it mean when animals and plants are relatives?

Protists are divided into haploid with one genome and diploid with two genomes. From an evolutionary point of view, it is believed that haploid protists evolved first. Diploid protists appear to have evolved by becoming diploid zygotes during the sexual reproduction process of haploid protists, and then living in diploid trophic forms for reasons such as the environment has not improved again. Having two genomes can be seen as the principle that it would be genetically more stable, just as two branches are more difficult to break than one branch.

Among them, haploid protists obtained multicellularization

factors and evolved into plants through algae, and diploid protists obtained multicellularization factors and evolved into animals. Since these are essentially protists except the multicellularity factor, multicellular organisms live as protists where the multicellularity factor is excluded. The method of forming gametes is the same whether they are haploid or diploid, and the generational alternation also is the same.

The sexual reproduction, reviewed in the chapter 4 above, is the case of haploid protist. The somatic cell is reproduced as it is, but it is divided into sperm and eggs, and spliced together to form a diploid zygote. Later, it undergoes meiosis to return to its usual trophic form, and in this state, reproduces by replicating somatic cells again. In other words, haploid protists alternate generations between the states of haploid and diploid during sexual reproduction.

Plants that have evolved by obtaining multicellularity factors follow the above path as they are, except for multicellularity in the case of sexual reproduction. That is, it alternates between the states of haploid and diploid, and multicellularization occurs in both haploid unicellular spores and diploid unicellular zygotes. Spores grow into multicellular gametophytes that form gametes, and diploid zygotic single cells grow into multicellular sporophytes. Since they are haploid protists in nature, diploid sporophytes undergo meiosis to revert to haploid unicellular spores.

The reason why single-celled diploid zygotes and single-celled haploid spores go through the growth process into multicellular organisms is that it is difficult to multicellularize in an instant, so they go through a step-by-step growth process. In addition, after the growth process, the reproductive maturity period that can reproduce safely is separated and arranged.

When diploid protists reproduce sexually, the way they form gametes is to reverse their evolutionary process. In other words, a haploid germ cell is formed by somatic meiosis directly from a diploid trophic somatic cell, and when two haploid germ cell sperm and egg are joined, it immediately returns to the diploid trophic form, so mitosis can be done in that state.

Since they basically live in a difficult environment to the extent that they have to live in a diploid trophic form, it is unlikely that the period of being a haploid germ cell will be long, so it is safe to say that generational alternation is almost meaningless.

Numerous biologists wonder about the secret of angiosperm evolution, that is, a diploid sporophyte absorbs a haploid gametophyte to become a diploid multicellular gametophyte like animals. All plants before the evolution of angiosperms, from seaweeds to gymnosperms, go through generational alternation of haploid gametophytes and diploid sporophytes, but angiosperms have settled their generational alternation as diploid gametophytes.

Even in ferns, diploid multicellular sporophytes are extremely dominant over haploid multicellular gametophytes, but gametophytes and sporophytes were separated. However, when it comes to gymnosperms, haploid multicellular gametophytes parasitize on diploid sporophytes. From meiosis to growth into gametophytes, formation and conjugation of gametes by gametophytes, and maturation of seeds, they are parasitized on sporophytes, and after the seeds are dispersed, they grow into diploid sporozoite multicellular organisms.

In angiosperms, diploid multicellular sporophytes absorbed the haploid gametophytes that were parasitic on the sporophytes, and evolved into diploid multicellular gametophytes. Thus, sperm and eggs, which are haploid gametes, are formed immediately through meiosis, and after conjugation, they directly connect to grow into diploid gametophytes by omitting the haploid gametophyte process.

In addition, the diploid chromosomes of these diploid gametophytes form germ cells, so they have been elevated to a very capable homologous chromosomal system. Homologous chromosomes are highly efficient genomic systems in which the more competent of the two alleles in a pair can be used. However, although the sporophytes of plants are diploids, they do not form germ cells as gametophytes, so unlike them, they cannot be said to be true homologous chromosomal systems.

Among multicellular organisms, diploid gametophytes are animals and angiosperms. And just as diploid protists have a short period of time as germ cells during sexual reproduction and generational alternation, thus has almost been eliminated, they produce sperm and eggs in their reproductive organs and their fertilized eggs immediately grow into diploid gametophyte multicellular organisms through which they completely eliminating generational alternation.

Their fertilized eggs, although developmental, are diploid gametophytes multicellular bodies. They are very capable homologous chromosomes with extremely complex genomic activity. Therefore, sufficient nutrients such as egg yolk and endosperm are stably supplied to the fertilized eggs until autotrophic is possible.

All multicellular organisms, such as animals and plants, are eukaryotes and share a nucleus containing the same genome, but in principle, the genes expressed in each cell are different. Judging by this, it seems that the essence of multicellular organisms is the communal life of individual cells. Protists have the ability to change the shape of their cells according to their life cycle, and the systematic growth ability of multicellular organisms, which are protists in nature, seems to come from this.

The reason why animals and plants are related is that in the days of protists long before the evolution of animals and plants, haploid protists and diploid protists were so close. Do you now understand why the germ cells of animals and angiosperms undergo meiosis, and why the germ cells of other plants undergo mitosis, and that they are all derived from somatic cells?

• • •

# 07

Biologists are most curious about the reason why homologous chromosomes are cross-recombined for meiosis when making sperm and eggs.

Previously, what animals and angiosperms have in common is the diploid gametophyte, but they are promoted to the homologous chromosome system. In the homologous chromosome system, extremely complex genetic activities are performed, such as using the one that is more advantageous for environmental adaptation among two alleles in a pair and this is the field where the complex Mendel's Laws of Inheritance are applied. This is because it enables segmentation and efficiency of organs by increasing developmental plasticity, and animals acquire motility early in evolution, and angiosperms account for more than 90% of all plants.

I will call this extremely capable homologous chromosome system the 'flower of evolution.' Because it is the genetic system that is the source of the 'genetic diversity' that every biologist admires. In other words, the possibility that a member of a species can uniquely bloom as a unique life with individuality was realized by this homologous chromosome system. Those who see life as a mere blind machine that copies selfish genes, I think they are ridiculous.

They form gametes through meiosis within the reproductive organs, and their fertilized eggs immediately grow into diploid gametophytes, ending the generational alternation. Nutrients are necessary for the development and germination of animal fertilized eggs and plant zygotes until autotrophic is possible, and the nutrients of animal eggs and the endosperm of double fertilization in angiosperms play the role. The formation of gametes by mitosis in haploid gametophyte plants to form diploid fertilized eggs, and the formation of asexual spores by meiosis in diploid sporophyte plants, cannot even be compared.

What is the reason for meiosis after crossing over and

recombination of parental homologous chromosomes during the formation of gametes in animals and angiosperms? If I say the conclusion, as the multicellularity factors, it is a phenomenon that diploid gametophytes, which essentially are protists, inherit the horizontal transfer of genes of prokaryotes once again, but modified and applied it according to the homologous chromosome system of diploid gametophytes multicellular organisms. If such cross-editing is not done, only gametes with the same genotype as the parents are produced, and the birth of genetically diverse individuals is impossible.

Therefore, the fact that diploid gametophytic multicellular organisms form gametes through meiosis, means the germ cell formation method works as essentially a diploid protist organism, while diploid gametophyte multicellularity works at the point of cross-editing homologous chromosomes. In other words, the phenomenon of editing by crossing homologous chromosomes when diploid gametophyte multicellular organisms form gametes through meiosis, is a phenomenon of inheriting the 'life cycle of gene horizontal transfer' of prokaryotes, and then modified and applied to fit diploid gametophyte multicellular organisms.

Horizontal gene transfer in prokaryotes acquired genes

for use in unexpected environments. But protists inheriting them during sexual reproduction was because they needed strong stability of cystic diploids in harsh environments.

Diploid gametophytes multicellular organisms inherited this again to acquire genetic diversity through chromosomal recombination and to enable individual adaptation to environment by using the most suitable genes. This has the effect of allowing a certain species to be survived and preserved no matter which way the environment changes. In other words, genetic diversity is the very purpose itself, but never a purpose of being exposed for natural selection!

All evolutions, aforementioned, have their distinguished purposes. All of them are precisely the results of their subjective adaptations according to their biological perception.

# 08

# What is the origin of sex, and that of the two sexes: male and female?

People might think the Creator made male and female of animals and they were there from the very beginning. In biology, however, it is a homework to be solved. In fact, I did not know either. But I never imagined that I would be the first of all mankind to give this explanation to others.

The reason for the evolution of sex (sexual reproduction) and male and female in multicellular organisms is, as discussed above, related to protists acquiring multicellularity factors to evolve into multicellular organisms for the advantage of survival.

When the habitat environment is harsh, haploid protists

divide somatic cells to form gametes, then connect two by two to become diploid. And when the environment improves, they return to the original trophic form through meiosis and reproduce by self-replication. This is but sexual reproduction.

In a diploid protist, the zygote has been forced to live in a diploid trophic form due to environmental factors. When they reproduce sexually, they turn their evolutionary process in reverse for meiosis of somatic cells to form haploid germ cells and to splice two by one to return to their usual trophic form, and then self-replicate. As we have seen above, the haploid evolved into plants and the diploid evolved into animals.

Protists, either through mitosis or meiosis, divide the reproductive cells from trophic somatic cells into sperm and eggs, forming only two of them simultaneously. Why? Jumping to the conclusion, this is to avoid deformity or infertility by preventing overzygosity through germ cell distinguishment.

In protists such as ciliates or in fungi such as yeasts and mushrooms, there are cases where more than two sexes exist. It seems clear since only two individuals of different sexes are bonded. In many multicellular organisms, abnormalities in the number of chromosomes cause malformations or infertility. For example, seedless watermelon is triploid, and Down's syndrome has three copies of chromosome 21.

Why are they multiple sexes, while multicellular organisms have two sexes? The big difference is whether they form gametes for the purpose of going straight to sexual reproduction. They live in the form of hyphae, which are usually considered as individuals, and connect with other hyphae of different sexes. Ciliates or yeasts reproduce asexually and only reproduce sexually with individuals of other sexes when the environment is unfavorable.

So, each individual acts as a kind of reproductive cell and connects other sexes except the same sex. This seems to be the natural phenomenon of sexual reproduction that seeks to take advantage of genetic diversity.

On the other hand, the sexual reproduction of protists, which evolved to survive when the environment is difficult and reproduce later when the environment is better, evolved with formal methods of reproduction that are distinct from asexual reproduction when in multicellular organisms.

Multicellular organisms inherited both asexual and sexual reproduction and both reproduction methods are modified and applied according to the system of multicellular organisms. Cuttings, for example, are asexual reproduction that only work for multicellular organisms.

Sexual reproduction became a more fundamental and routine method of reproduction than asexual reproduction in multicellular organisms. This seems to be because sexual reproduction is so beneficial to multicellular organisms. Plants can adapt to form that are more suitable to the environment throughout their life as both haploid gametophytes and diploid sporophytes. Animals and angiosperms appear to have genetic diversity due to the homologous chromosomal system.

When multicellular organisms reproduce sexually, the pattern differs between plants and animals. As we have seen, plants including gymnosperms alternate between gametophyte and sporophyte generations. Multicellularization occurs in a diploid zygote where two gametes are joined, and grows into a diploid sporophyte. Multicellularity occurs in the haploid spores produced by the sporophyte through meiosis, and grows into the haploid gametophytes that produce sperm and eggs by mitosis.

As animals and angiosperms are diploid gametophytes, and have cleared the generational alternation, multicellularization occurs in the diploid zygote (fertilized egg) of two meiotic gametes, which immediately grow into gametophytes. They again produce haploid gametes through meiosis, that are, sperm and eggs.

Protists are sexless because they divide single-celled somatic cells to produce reproductive cells. In multicellular organisms, the reason why the early organisms are hermaphroditic, or monoecism, is because they seem to be direct descendants of protists without sex, but they must form sperm and eggs simultaneously like protists.

As animals evolve, male and female gametophytes evolve into separate bodies. This is because animals move and live by motility. But we must not forget that the male and female evolve simultaneously. Animals evolve in the order of sponges, cnidarians, flatworms, nematodes, annelids, echinoderms, mollusks, and arthropods. Sponges and cnidarians live a fixed life, and from flatworms move. Sponges and cnidarians, such as anemones, are hermaphroditic and release sperm and eggs at the same time to cross-fertilize.

Flatworms, linear animals and even annelids are usually hermaphroditic, Two individuals meet, exchange sperm and eggs with each other through mating, and both lay eggs. Flatworms are hermaphroditic, and through penis fencing, the penis is first stabbed into the opponent's body, releasing sperm and escaping, and the stabbed one lays eggs. In hermaphroditic snails, the larger snail accepts sperm and lays eggs, and both exchange sperm and eggs if they are similar in size.

Since animals cross fertilize, there are many inconveniences in mating if they are hermaphroditic. Thus, from echinoderms, it evolves into gonochorism, and females and males of the same species produce eggs and sperm at the same time, and meet and breed when they mate. Whether a plant is a hermaphrodite or a dioecism, this is also a phenomenon of simultaneous evolution of both sexes. Due to the nature of plants that live on the ground, cross fertilization is basic even if they have evolved into hermaphrodites to overcome the difficulty of fertilization.

So, sex evolved as part of a method for fertilizing sperm and eggs produced by female and male gametophytes. In other words, in multicellular organisms, the multicellular male gametophytes that form sperm are male, and the multicellular female gametophytes that form eggs are female.

So, the reason why multicellular organisms, which are essentially protists, evolved into only male and female sexes is the same as why protists only form sperm and eggs as reproductive cells. In other words, the origin of the two sexes, male and female, is a measure to prevent over-splicing for the purpose of avoiding deformity and infertility!

Sperm and eggs were distinguished when protists form them, and as evolution progressed, they were distinguished by the presence or absence of cytoplasm. This is to facilitate the detection of both gametes, enabling rapid and accurate fertilization.

Eukaryotes, such as multicellular organisms, have genetic information necessary for survival and reproduction in chromosomes in the nucleus. Spermatozoa seem to have evolved by removing the cytoplasm, since the cytoplasm causes collision that hinder rapid conjugation. As a result, the egg has cytoplasm containing nutrients such as cytoplasm or egg yolk to accept sperm for fertilization of reproductive cells.

In other words, female gametophytes, such as insects and mammals, play the role of storing sperm in preparation for fertilization or protecting fertilized eggs or fetuses, that is, conceiving, only because females produce eggs. How did the female come to produce eggs? As we have seen above, it is only by chance that it is responsible for the production of gametes containing cytoplasm, that is, eggs.

Therefore, female pregnancy can only be said to be a sacrificial effort from the species point of view. This also is the reason that females of all animals miscarry when their survival is threatened by pregnancy. Even after the birth, there are quite a few cases of abandoning the young when the mother's (or the parents') survival is threatened.

Spotted eagle rays immediately abort if stressed during pregnancy. Cape fur seals in South Africa abort in groups when food is scarce. Lack of sunlight causes the fruit to whiten. There are many strong predators in the sand tiger shark's habitat, so it cannot survive unless the newborn baby is big. The baby that wakes up first eats all the babies that are born later, even the unhatched chicks, and grows to a size of 1 meter before being born. Male poison dart frogs in South America raise their young by carrying them one by one in 5 to 6 water holes on plants for 6 weeks. Each time the female follows and lays unfertilized eggs as food. I also saw a Porcupine couple with a lower rank in the zoo abandoning their offspring to survive.

Can you see the rules by which lives live above? It is but the phenomenon of 'pre-survival, post-reproduction'. In other words, survival is the top priority for all organisms. Reproduction is carried out as long as it does not infringe on survival. When necessary, even the reproductive behavior is used for survival.

Sexual reproduction of protists also evolved in the process of 'pre-survival, post-reproduction'. They first seek to survive when the environment is unfavorable, such as in winter, and then reproduce when the environment improves later. The above principles are generally followed for each species of multicellular organisms to use either sexual or asexual reproduction.

# 09

# Pre-survival, post-reproduction?

All living things survive first, and reproduction is done within a line that does not interfere with survival. Survival is the top priority for all organisms. Reproduction is carried out as long as it does not infringe on survival. When necessary, even the reproductive behavior is used for survival.

Prokaryotes cannot reproduce without nutrients. Some prokaryotes form 'endospores' to survive when the environment is unfavorable. Unusually, they partially use the binary method known as breeding, in which genomes are cloned and aggregated.

Even when protists reproduce asexually, they prepare very carefully for the reproductive period after the survival period. The evolution of sexual reproduction by protists is also a product of evolution in the process of surviving in harsh environments and reproducing after the environment improves.

Organisms establish ecological niches to avoid competition and to survive stably. Does not competition endanger survival? In this sense, all organisms form species and survive and reproduce as species units. The principle of 'pre-survival, post-reproduction' flows at the basis of all living things: speciation, the breeding method of each species, the reasons for the behavior of individual organisms, and the marriage system of humans.

'Pre-survival, post-reproduction' is the reason why the reproductive maturity stage is arranged in the growth process of multicellular organisms including insects and vertebrates, all animals, and all plants; and why, even after sexual maturity, breeding is performed by species in the safest time and way depending on the seasonal factors of the habitat environment; and why high-ranking vertebrate females that live in groups such as wolves participate in breeding. This principle also works in the evolution of plants such as angiosperms of course.

Human female go through menopause at an older age.

Some primates remain sterile for about two years after reaching sexual maturity. This is to prevent pregnancy and childbirth in earlier or old age from threatening the survival of the mother. There seems to be a reason behind the prohibition of interracial marriage in primitive tribes and of incest generally forbidden: to prevent the possibility of genetic defects. The same principle also works behind the marriage systems: the monogamy to prevent love competition between men and women and the polygamy in extremely poor environments.

The Industrial Revolution rapidly reorganized the society. It gave birth to Romanticism while dismantled large families into small families. Some men felt a huge burden of the patriarchical duty and started to refuse it. The phenomenon of homosexuality might have come and evolved from this. In other words, it is possible that raising a family and supporting a spouse and children was considered an excessive duty.

Women's contraception and abortion already have their origins in the times of Egypt, Greece and Rome. In modern times, abortion were allowed as a basic right of the women who abort with medical safeness when she could not give birth and to avoid risking their lives through illegal abortion. Abortion is an act carried out when the birth of a child severly risks survival of the mother. The same principle lies behind the phenomenon of avoiding marriage and childbirth which has become a social problem these days.

Species also divide into collective life and independent life for the advantage of survival. It is advantageous for herbivores to live in groups to guard against predators. When members compete to determine rankings for eating food or breeding, competition occurs only when the size of the individuals is similar. This is to ensure that the small-sized bodies are not easily killed or injured, while the similar-sized bodies compete and establish the ranks to prevent a new fight every time they meet so they maintain survival. A species that lives independently and determines its own territory is the same principle. In other words, all living organisms refrain from unnecessary competition and coexist peacefully. This is the Lamarckian view of the world. The Darwinian view of life that the '10,000 creatures compete for 10,000 creatures', therefore, must be said to be completely wrong.

# 10

So, the different shapes of female and male are the result of use and disuse of organs in the 'pre-survival, post-reproduction' order?

Since animals are mobile, they behave in such a way that they first survive and reproduce later in their ecological niche. Their sexual dimorphism accurately reflects that outcome. Darwin wondered why male peacocks have colorful tails and why only queen ants and bees reproduce. To conclude, both are the result of 'pre-survival, post-reproduction'. Darwin prophesied that his theory of evolution would collapse the day someone came along who could properly explain the evolution of ants.

Since multicellular organisms contain protists factors, the speciation of multicellular organisms can be understood by this. During speciation, male and female individual members become the center due to multicellular organisms. But the reason why they always occur in species units is because they are unicellular protists in nature. Therefore, the definition of a species should be: 'a population sharing a common way of survival and reproduction'.

The reason why only the queen is in charge of reproduction in ants, bees, clownfish and naked mole rats is as follows: their ecological position is closed, and in this case, if each female participates in reproduction beyond survival, the ecological position cannot be maintained and even a stable survival opportunity can be threatened. So, from the breeding method, 'pre-survival, post-reproduction' worked.

It is a declaration that a creature is a being that values its single chance of survival above all else, and that breeding is a lower priority.

In hyenas, females are extremely dominant over males. This is a result of their ecological status as omnivores, and females fiercely protect themselves and their cubs from males. Seahorses, which evolved from fish, live in places with fast currents, wrapping their tails around water plants.

If they fertilize sperm and eggs by spraying them into the water like fish, not only sperm and eggs but also fertilized eggs will be swept away by the current. In addition, if a female that produces eggs with yolk becomes pregnant, the female's survival will be endangered, so the male protects the fertilized eggs by putting them in a nursery bag as if pregnant.

Female catfish in the Amazon, which live in places with extremely fast currents, instantly swallow the sperm released from the male's genital organs, and fertilize with the waiting eggs in the body cavity, and protrude the fertilized eggs out of the cloacal cavity immediately. This also is the same principle.

The reason why male peacocks and birds of paradise are exceptionally beautiful is that they have a rich environment for survival, such as abundant food. As there is no problem in survival without any special effort and the female even takes care of incubation alone, males just focus on breeding, considering the nature of birds that they are highly intelligent and agile.

All of them act in the order of 'pre-survival, post-reproduction' in their respective ecological statuses, and as a result, the use and disuse of the organ is made accordingly.

Thus, speciation being completed in all animal species, male and female simultaneously acquire survival traits first, and subsequently, they also simultaneously acquire the reproductive traits like the reproductive system separately in the ecological status.

In other words, the male and female of all species evolve simultaneously, whether they are hermaphroditic or gonochorism. In Lamarckism, male and female evolve simultaneously, but Darwinism does not explain this simultaneous evolution of male and female.

In principle, acquisition of traits by use and disuse can result in simultaneous changes by simultaneous use of various body organs. For example, a change in a bird's beak can be accompanied by changes in its wings, body, and legs for physical balance of the body.

Modularity of toolkit gene and switch gene combinations by Evolutionary Developmental Biology (EVODEVO), neuroplasticity enabling extremely rapid changes in sensory and motor neurons, and Barbara McClintock's discovery of the 'jumping gene', indicates that simultaneous evolution of all organs of the body is possible. If they are for Darwinian natural selection, they are over-specified.

Stem cells, which are somatic cells, seem to play this

leading role in animals, and they pass on acquired traits to reproductive cells. After the death of a man, who received a woman's heart transplant, the chromosomes of the man's heart cells were examined, and 10% of the sex chromosomes were the original XY of the man, not the XX of the transplanted woman. Scientists inferred that stem cells played the role.

This conclusion agrees with the fact that multicellular organisms, which are protists in nature, will also produce reproductive cells by division of somatic cells, just like protists. Is not this a typical 'pre-survival, post-reproduction'?

• • •

# 11

# What does it mean that the biological two sexes of animals are not the same as social sex (gender)?

The reason why the biological sex of multicellular organisms is two sexes, male and female, can be understood by the fact that their essence is a single-celled protist. In other words, protists formed only two reproductive cells, a sperm and an egg, as a measure to prevent oversplicing for the purpose of avoiding deformities and infertility. Multicellular organisms also inherited this and evolved their reproductive cells to form only an egg and a sperm. As a result, they evolved into female gametophytes that produce eggs and male gametophytes that produce sperm.

The definition of a species is 'a population sharing a common way of survival and reproduction'. Here, the method of survival and reproduction is in the order of 'pre-survival, post-reproduction', and like we have studied already, sexual dimorphism is the very result.

On the other hand, since each species adapts reproductively in each ecological position, and even if they have two biological sexes by the evolutionary process, their social sex (gender) cannot necessarily be said to be two male and female. The question of how many genders can appear in one species is reappeared in the form of specific adaptations of individuals. And this is but their true gender.

Male lizards from California's Central Valley have three genders, identified by the color of their necks: the yellow neck mates with all females in its territory; the blue neck maintains monogamy, and the orange neck roams quietly and attracts solitary females. It seems that it is impossible to breed with only one gender because the habitat is very wide and the environment changes from year to year. Blue ball rockfish males also have three similar genders. There are quite a few species with multiple genders, both male and female.

Meanwhile, American serratum plant easily goes back

and forth between the male and female every year. Even in animals, there are not a few species that change sex. When the reproductive female clownfish dies, the largest male becomes the female, and the largest of the immature males matures and mates with it. In the polygamous coral fish 'blue- backed cleaning wrasse', the male is the largest and the rest are female. When this male dies, the largest of the females will change sex to become a male.

In animals, there are many female-like males and male-like females, depending on the species. Great Painted-snipe is monogamous and unlike other birds, females are as colorful and aggressive as males. They approach the males first, mate with them, and then lay eggs for the males to incubate. It is a typical male-like female. There are quite a few species of birds with female-like males and male-like females. All of these adaptations are understood as the result of 'pre-survival, post-reproduction' in their ecological niche.

In conclusion, the biological duality of sex is not a priori, but it is only distinguished by 'hyperjunction prevention measures' when one species reproduces sexually. Depending on the ecological niche, several social genders can evolve when it is inappropriate to reproduce with a typical male and female sex. Depending on the need, the same individual may be sex-converted into a female and a male. Also, additional adaptations may emerge in which individuals of one sex take on the character and appearance of the opposite sex.

What are the adaptive benefits of being transgender? Transgender stands on the extension of biological adaptation, but it seems to be a phenomenon that is possible only in the highly evolved species: Sapiens. Individual and social members... for whatever reason, individuals who live in  a world where biological men and women contain the characteristics of each gender and live together are bound to influence each other. Once a species with an ecological niche is established, survival and reproductive adaptations become inseparable to the point of being almost indistinguishable. That may be why Darwin's natural and sexual selection worked for a long time.

Have you heard of the legendary Amazoness? Why did they do that? Wouldn't it be better to want to be a man instead of just being a manly female warrior? Conversely, what about men? Shouldn't men and women be so eager to be like each other that they recognize their own gender identity as the opposite sex? As a result of the fruit fly genome experiment, no matter how female the body is, if one of the critical focuses in the brain is male, it behaves as a male and vice versa. For the same reason, shouldn't the same sex be attracted to the same sex? Abnormal? What is normal then?

To sum up the evolution of animals, it is the result of 'pre-survival, post-reproductive behavior and the resultant use and disuse of organs' in the ecological niche. What does it mean? It means that all living things are beings whose top priority is but survival. In other words, depending on the individual, whether it wants reproduction or not is not as important as survival but optional. All living things are respected for the reason for being alive. This is why ants, bees, clownfish and naked mole rats do not have any problems of adapting even if they do not reproduce like queen females. In many mammals, males and females with lower ranks do not participate in reproduction, and this also has nothing to do with natural selection because it is not a problem evolutionarily!

The biological implication of animals adapting according to their internal will by the use and disuse of their organs means that the subject of evolution is neurons, not genes. What is a gene? By the formation of new ecological niches and, consequently, by the action of neurons, the adaptive traits acquired with use and disuse in organs enter the pool of alleles. That is, it is an automated program for maximum efficiency in the unfolding of adaptive traits by offspring. Adaptation of organisms must be done immediately, so descendants inherit the traits of their ancestors and start off. Once it becomes a genetic trait, then the allele will float in the form and be able to appear in anyone.

It also means that biological adaptation can happen right now, if necessary. In other words, we are the beneficiaries of evolution and, at the same time, performers of evolution. In all of the above, it seems that the true identity of every animal is in its neurons, not its genes. Therefore, it is believed that an individual's identity should not be determined differently just because a gene, or sex chromosome, was expressed in a different direction.

Of course, there are inevitably limits to the social adaptations of our species as social animals, and that is why the law has evolved. Humans are social animals, so the first thing to do is not to infringe on the lives or rights of others. But why should others interfere with the evolutionary phenomenon in which an individual expresses his unique identity as life in society? As far as I know, this is the true nature of the honest adaptation of life according to the Lamarckian view of life.

The biological nature of feminism can also be understood in this way. This means that the essence of our species lies in the survival and adaptive traits of both sexes but not in the reproductive traits. This is because, if the true nature of an animal species is to be found in the genome, it must be found in the autosomes that represent survival traits, not the sex chromosomes that represent biological male and female sex distinction, which are reproductive traits. In accordance with the principle of 'pre-survival, post-reproduction, all living things survive first as life and reproduction is accompanied after. This throws an important question: What is lacking in women in the nature of our species?

As an extension of that, you might find it surprisingly easy to solve when the marriage and birth rates become a social problem by applying this principle. First of all, the overall living environment should be improved, and the distribution of social costs of pregnancy, childbirth and childrearing should be balanced between society and men and women. In particular, women should not be disadvantaged or unfairly treated in balancing this.

**12**

• • •

## This is something Darwinian biologists would be astonished?

Life is a machine for selfish genes to replicate themselves? Is not it tautology? Where did it go, the vitality inherent in life? What is the point of replicating if life has no value as beautifully blooming? If life is a mere breeding machine, why do you think there was an evolution of life? Shouldn't the earth be teeming with the same life? How can nature exercise a selection that is necessarily artificial? How can we imagine that the 3.8 billion year history of life is just a result of chance?

Has there ever been a time in history when gods did not take care of humans? Did not they have even the slightest reverence for the gods who is saving billions of people around the world even now? God is a delusion? How can they have no doubts about their own knowledge while assaulting creationist dogma? Are not they the best intellectuals who have dealt with knowledge that corresponds to almost exclusively the level of truth since the dawn of science? Have not the believers been blindly loyal to Charles Darwin for 100 years, serving humans instead of God?

What did they do when religious people persecute aborted women and sexual minorities? Rather, what do they think about the fact that solid genetic determinism has become a tool of persecution wielded by religious people? It was not enough to blaspheme the holy God, but tossing it out as non- existent? Did not they make people orphans, not freeing them from God, but separating them from the position of precious children of the noble God? Do scientists really consider themselves qualified to teach people?

**13**

• • •

## Jesus' lawyer? Should we believe it?

When Jesus appeared to me at the age of 20 and said, "The truth will set you free," having never read the Bible, I concluded that 'the truth is not in a world without God, but in a world with God'. Right away, I began to believe in God. However, I was not zealous because I was not accustomed to the life of faith. Eventually came to atheism, and one day in my late 40s, I heard the voice of the God of the Old Testament, "Humans, stop being arrogant," and I have been acknowledging the existence of God again ever since.

My profession is a lawyer, but I suffered all my life because it did not fit my aptitude. One day in my thirties, while I was pessimistic about my inability to leave, I heard the voice of Jesus, "You wanted it." I was very surprised. I remembered praying for a vow while preparing for the second round of the bar exam: "If You let me pass, I'll believe You better." I barely passed because I got a high score at a question about a civil law case. And it sounded like Jesus said to me, "I have made your prayers come true because you wanted it." Maybe it was an extension of this event in series that in the spring of 2021, when I was washing my hands after the hard work on the biological principles of sexual minorities, I heard the voice of Jesus saying, "We made Sung-hee a lawyer for this." Then I cried and cried for how long I do not know.

While I was writing the newly discovered modes of existence of all living things such as 'Evolution of the Sex and the Two Sexes: Male and Female' and 'Pre-Survival, Post-Reproduction' of Lamarckism, I found that my experiences went beyond the personal. I realized that I was a being who heard the voice of God, and the importance of my duty was recognized by the people's response, saying, "If it is about the origin of male and female, it is the work of the Creator."

I wrote the 380-page book in one full year. Starting with a mechanism called 'life history inheritance' in August 2020, I ended 'evolution of sex' in 6 months. But because of my nickname 'Lamarck's daughter', the book eventually was published in August 2021 containing the Lamarck's theory of evolution. I faced hundreds of questions over the course of a year, always getting answers in sentence form, but never more than a day later. If it was a difficult question, I woke up with an answer-sentence from my next sleep. In the end, I could not help but conclude that I wrote this book with God.

At the end of the book, while dealing with 'God's scientific nature', I had the feeling that Jesus would return and I would be in charge of that task, but I did not know what form it would be. From then on, I called myself 'God's messenger' and 'Latter-day John the Baptist'. I was also aware that I had been entrusted with the mission of integrating religion and science, but I had no idea what it would look like.

But for such a huge discovery, the repercussions were too small. Charles Darwin's place in biology was no less than that of Jesus Christ in Christianity. The Christian side took issue with the fact that abortion and LGBTI are scientific phenomena. I faced the reality and had to take it one step at a time. Because it was about the 'Resurrection of Lamarck', and subsequently in a hope of attracting attention from French Embassy Seoul, I published my research in the December 2021 issue of monthly PowerKorea, which is distributed to various embassies in Seoul. On Christmas Day of the same year, a "report on discovery" was sent to

30 destinations, including science magazines, biological societies, and some embassies. This meant that humans were the first to give a birthday present to the birth of 'Jesus', who has ever cared for us. But there was no answer.

People around me said that I would not be recognized before I died. I wailed, as the year was closing, "You Said that You have been waiting for me and You are the science. But people are just laughing at me." Immediately came the rebuking voice of Jesus. "I was crucified for proclaiming the truth. How many days have you done?" I fell down and cried. On 31 December, the God of the Old Testament appeared in my dream with a voice, and assured me of my righteousness, saying, "Evil spirits will never appear in your dreams."

The year turned to 2022. I was advised to pair up with a biology professor and publish the article in a science journal. So I prayed to find a co-worker. But Jesus said, "You have me, and you are my co-worker." I said in prayer, "I see, my Lord. I will closely follow you. Guide me your way." It was around this time that I came to know the ongoing abortion rights case in the U.S. Federal Supreme Court. I knew right away that I was going to do something about it. From then on, I began to call myself "God's lawyer," considering that I came to defend the scientific nature of God and the primary mode of existence of all living things including the Sapiens.

I started studying about God, abortion and homosexuality. This is because God, aborted women, and sexual minorities have no choice but to stand on the same side. Just as a woman conceives an unwelcome child and people struggle with their identity, the perfect God goes hand in hand with human imperfection. I intended to prepare my arguments, but my studies did not go deep all at once. Also, I was suddenly called to be vice president of the Korean Bar Association. The ruling of the Court was leaked and protests against it lined up, but on June 24, the verdict was pronounced without change.

On June 29, 2022, while on the phone with a friend, I felt the need to send a formal letter to the French Embassy Seoul this time. I thought it lightly at first, but on July 5, I heard the very serious voice of Jesus, "If you neglect this opportunity, you will miss it." Immediately, I started digging into French history including the French Revolution, President Macron, Jeanne d'Arc, and Ernest Renan's "Life of Jesus" for three months. The contents of my study were summarized under the title 'The 21st Century is the time of Macron France'.

It was sent to the embassy on September 30, along with a 'report of discovery' and a 'book introduction' in English. On September 27th, an article appeared about President Macron's state visit to the United States on December 1st, so I thought it was timely.

While waiting for their reply, I began to read through the 4 Gospels of the New Testament in order to know the natural voice of Jesus from October. Included in the reading were some of the historical books about the time of Jesus and of prominent theologians. I used a Bible App in English, and I was surprised when I read John 14-16 in which Jesus repeatedly said that he would send 'The Advocate as my representative'. "This is me!" I said. In Korean, it means 'a lawyer who represents Jesus'. In the Korean Bible, it is translated as "Holy Spirit the Comforter." For me, the context made it clear that it was me. Jesus also said, "I knew you would come looking for Me as Truth." It was full of meaning as it was the completion of "The truth will set you free," which I heard directly from Jesus when I was 20 years old.

I realized that being called to the honorable Korean Bar Association meant that Jesus was asking for reconciliation with me, who had been at odds with the lawyer's job all my life. I also realized that there was one more thing in the voice of Jesus I heard in my 30s, "You wanted it." Even though it was impossible for me to study at college in Seoul due to family circumstances, Jesus Responded to me who murmured, "Horses go to Jeju-do, people go to Seoul." I then earned a judicial scholarship. "Did you have a hard time? But the position of lawyer I sent you to is such an honorable position. You have worked hard (including the work on the book)." said Jesus. Lawyers are an honorable profession that establishes justice in society no matter what people say. It was a job that was differentiated from the priest who served God in the distant days. The time to reconcile with my past and solidify my identity continued, and I do not know how much tears I shed during the course.

It became clear that the French Embassy was not going to do anything, and the time for President Macron's visit to the United States approached day by day. I sought out a few newspapers that would interview me with respect to my good intention of helping American women. Since science is fundamentally difficult, and especially since my findings were non-existent, no one understood my arguments. So I thought that if anyone was to interview me, I would write down what I wanted to say in the form of an interview. And the title was exactly the same as the title of this book.

However, Jesus seemed to have a different idea, and during lunch on November 13, He said, "That will not work." Indeed, newspapers did not respond at all.

Around the end of November, I started working on my book based on what I had found out so far. As if things were going differently, since Christmas, I could not stop thinking, "I must prepare for the Second Coming of Christ." Like John the Baptist welcomed Jesus, I should prepare for His Second Coming. And I thought it a good idea if my self-interview was translated into English. I thought about sending it to a translation company, but decided to try it myself with Google Translate. And it was the right decision; it has been modified countless times.

The translation was done on January 19th. Running alone for the past 7 years has been difficult, but I could not quit. Who will help American women if I quit, and how can Christ come? I needed extraordinary energy, and I remembered the bravery of animals I had seen on NAT GEO WILD and BBC EARTH for many years. Eagles, leopards, and snakes. I had to be relentless like them.

In the middle of the night, I suddenly felt the need to tell the world's leading biologists that 'Christ is returning'. These are the star authors of books that I came to know while studying biology. I sent them an e-mail all at once. After that, I was driving around downtown Seoul in a car, and tears welled up. I cried and cried in the car as I released all my complaints and gratitude to my Jesus...

When I woke up the next afternoon, I felt like I was going crazy. I plunged into despair. There was no reply from anyone, and I wondered when on earth someone would recognize me. I soon threw away the manuscript of the book I had been writing for a month, and thought of writing a new book based on the contents of my interview in Korean-English translation. I immediately rushed into it and it went on till now. Auspicious dreams or signs are continuing. But I do not believe it. Because, the essence of faith today is 'reasoning'. Instead of waiting for the words of Christ, I try harder to put into practice His will of pursuing the truth. The Word will be given when I need it most.

Ah! One more thing to mention! On February 3, while sending my book to a Korean who is working hard to promote friendship between Korea and France, I had the courage to send it to President Emmanuel Macron and First Lady Brigitte Macron. I carefully signed my book in Korean, French and English with Google Translate, and sent it along with other materials. My pride is higher than ever!

# 14

# When most intellectuals are atheists, who say 'God is a scientific being'?

Called as the saint of the poor, Mother Teresa was a great Catholic nun who was posthumously canonized as a saint. I happened to learn that she was not able to pray because she could not feel the God. I was curious. How come the ardent believer like her could fall into a doubt? Was it that she might be influenced by the cruelty in the scene ministry works and the atheism of Western intellectuals? Is there really no God? Then what are the billions of people who believe in gods? What is the truth? When I was about to finish the book around the early summer in 2021, I heard the voice of the God in the Old Testament saying "I have been waiting for you. I am the science." And I thought it was time to face it. No one but by me!

Thomas Kuhn said in his book <The Structure of Scientific Revolutions>, that a prerequisite for a scientific revolution is the realization of functional deficiencies that cause crisis in both political and scientific development. Are we, humans, also not biological beings? A transgender soldier committed suicide after being forcibly discharged. A pastor was suspended for two years for throwing flowers of blessing to homosexuals. Women in many states of the U.S., the privacy that no one needs to know like abortion is violated by the Supreme Court Justices. Is not this barbarism, not a comedy or tragedy?

Humanity has made progress since the beginning of the day. But why is this sudden stop, or even retreat I might have to say? Does not this mean that the Darwinian paradigm that has driven the modern biology is wrong? Darwinists quarrel with the believers in creationism, and the evolutionary psychologists, a sub-disciple group of sociobiology nested on the genetic determinism, fight against feminists. Is not science the study of natural phenomena without judgement? Why then they scream that there is no God or God is an illusion? We have no choice but to rely on scientific theories when it comes to the order of nature. In this situation, can politics play its role?

How did God appear in human history? The bottom line is, God evolved along with Homo sapiens, who appeared through the evolution of language along the line of evolution of the genus Homo. That is, since God and man are twins, God is as real as we are. Let us infer its specific progress.

During the course of human evolution, the size of the brain increased to such an extent that, scientists express, it expanded for only 2.5 million years. The reason might be that they seem to have used their brain constantly, in order to steadily expand and advance the range and degree of awareness of environmental elements, and master them. It is interpreted to mean that the more the next generation, the more complex and detailed environmental factors were experienced from birth to death, and they memorize. In other words, mankind has adapted by steadily increasing 'knowledge (non-linguistic perceptual memory)' through environmental factors. There would have been almost nothing unknown about environmental factors for their brain to be reached to the size of modern humans today, and as a result, language evolution would have been possible.

The evolution of language may have begun with naming

objects and actions. Using these names in conversations produces knowledge (ideas) by which we think, act and live. Verbalization is not simply about gaining a piece of knowledge, but it is a task that essentially requires understanding. Then, in what way they understood objects? Through 'personification', they might have regarded them like they would act like us. Are not all the animals and plants around us alive like us? Does not even night and day change? Also, it seems that a distinction has been made between the thinking beings, that is, the ideal us (soul), and the real us (body) as objects. Because when we die, we become like inanimate objects.

However, if we look at the nature of language evolution as an extension of biological evolution, it is merely a translation of all biometric information (sensory information, emotional/ cognitive information, and motor information) using a tool called language. It is obvious compared to mammals and primates without language. In other words, other animals perceive and react to things and actions, but they accept and respond only to the image and behavior of things themselves, without translating them through language like we do. Then, for Sapiens, ideas (knowledge) are based on reality, and the concept of their sum is the same no matter how abstract and complicated it may seem. So, for Homo sapiens, 'concept is reality!'

The essence of language evolution is 'translating information into language', but due to this translation work, the original speed of life has been lost, and as a result, we cannot easily catch even mosquitoes with our bare hands. In Benjamin Libet's 'free will' experiment, the brain responds faster than the moment a person recognizes the will to do something, and the reason seems to be the difference in translation time. The upward and downward paths in our brains were also divided according to whether they were translated or not. The downward path is the implementation of the translated information, and the upward path is to react first and translate later in life-threatening emergency situations. We live in consciousness and unconsciousness, and 'consciousness' is interpreted to mean biometric information translated into language, and 'unconsciousness' means biometric information (memories, etc.) that are not translated and are locked inside.

Because of language, mankind was able to become Homo sapiens, or wise beings, for the first time. However, the evolution of Sapiens came with a fatal weakness: the more we know, the more the appearance of ignorance accompanies us, and the world of the ignorance grows more. The life of animals without language translation does not escape spontaneity and presence. However, 'Ignorance', which appeared due to the evolution of language, causes fear and anxiety from time to time. It would have been an unprecedented challenge for Sapiens, who lived by dominating the environment. The inevitable solution to this was interpreted (considered) that 'some living being, that is, a transcendental being' had done some kind of manipulation, and embraced Ignorance, and thus trying to regain a sense of stability. In other words, if you admit that you do not know what you do not know, you can feel comfortable at first.

The transcendent functioned as a personality from the beginning. Mankind started from the habit of personifying all things, and therefore, the existence that manipulates something was inevitably artificial. Moreover, it was perceived as much more powerful than us. Because such is its origin, and it treats things people do not know and cannot understand. So, such beings always think and act differently than we do, and it is not easy to predict them. In other words, God is indispensable to human adaptation, and is just as real as we are. God and us are twins born from the same mother.

As mankind made progress from initial primitive states

to cities, societies developed and the civilizations advanced. Correspondingly, the transcendent evolved from spirits or evil spirits to multiple gods in charge of nature, and then to a single god. The scope of each transcendent's control included a plan to cope with the omens and misfortunes according to each individual and systemic needs of each society and various incidents. In addition, God had to give answers to human requests and questions such as the beginning and end of the world including the earth and the sky, the origin of all living things and humans, life and death, the problem of suffering, good and evil, sin and punishment or forgiveness, and all things that are not easily known cognitively including the present world and the transcendental world.

The use of gods has not diminished in the present age with cutting edge technologies. Rather, personal utility is more added. Are not the gods our only friends to whom we can confide everything? How can we live without God? This is the religious adaptation unique to Homo sapiens, and it is the most humane and at the same time the ultimate scientific adaptation.

However, it should be noted that just because human beings live by the most powerful tool of thought, 'the language', does not mean that they have become perfect like gods. In other words, verbalization made us live by translating various biometric information into language, but the nature of us is still just 'talking animals'. We are not exempted from animal nature just because we have come to distinguish between good and evil and some other things by the power of language. Humans, too, are merely beings that have evolved through mammals and primates. This is but the biological meaning of the saying that human beings are born with 'original sin'. Therefore, God does not leave human beings until human beings become perfect like God.

Since God's evolutionary path is like this, God has never abandoned us and has always been by our side. When we call upon God, He immediately sends us the Holy Spirit. God will never ever abandon humans. If God is not felt, it is not because God does not exist or because God has abandoned man. On the contrary, it is because humans have left God or abandoned it by judging that it does not exist. This is the view of God from the Lamarckian paradigm. If Mother Teresa had known this, would she not have returned again and again to take Christ's hand?

We live with language as a tool means we live in concept. Without concept, we have neither love nor justice not to mention name, time, place and of course appointment. In the same sense and with equal importance, God is real in our lives. Wittgenstein, who used language as a tool for philosophy, said, "The limits of my language mean the limits of my world." Language as an excellent tool of thought inevitably unfolds ideal theories. Therefore, since we live in language, paradigms are so important because we are confined within the framework of this systematic theory. However, I think scientists should tell people that no matter how complex an idea is, it reflects reality. This is because the beginning of the idea was 'reality', and in its essence it is still the same. If we keep this in mind, we will never get lost.

• • •

# 15

# What does it mean that Jesus returns?

In April and May, 2021, as I entered the closing of my book on realizing the 'new evolutionary theory and the science of god', my old memories came back. I hardly lived a religious life despite the fact that I received evangelism directly from Jesus at the age of 20. The impression I received from the Bible, which I first encountered during the evangelism process, was that God is similar to humans. I did not know whether God was an object, a soul, or all things but God was similar to man in the way He was jealous and angry. So, I accepted God at once and put aside books of Nietzsche who said 'God is dead'. Nevertheless, I have not been friends with Jesus for a long time.

When I called "God," prayers came out, but I never thought that the god was "Jesus." Yes, from the beginning I did not think that Jesus was the descent of the god of the Old Testament. Because, I was able to pray just by acknowledging the existence of God, and I felt that 'God was in human instinct'. That year, on Christmas day, I came back home on my way to church. Because I wondered one thing about 'The Virgin Mary': "A virgin gave birth to a child without sexual intercourse? That is a lie." But my curiosity also was an opportunity to think about the human-side of Jesus: his troubles must have been deep because he did not know who his father was, and thus his identity!

In my early 40s, I became an avid believer for about a year to overcome severe depression. The fact that 'Jesus hung on the cross instead of me' helped me a lot. But still not knowing the true identity of Jesus made me forget Him again as I had passed through the depression. At some point, influenced by the knowledge of scientists that 'God is in the molecule', I fell into atheism. Then, in my mid-40s, when I heard the voice of God in the Old Testament telling people to stop being arrogant, I started thinking about God again little by little.

In 2020, I read Renan's "Life of Jesus," which I had been eager to read for a long time. In the 1800s, Renan saw Jesus as thoroughly human, and the human Jesus was truly amazing. I was the one who must have changed over time. I could not stop crying throughout the reading. In the early summer of 2021, as an extension of "God's Science," I read the 4 Gospels of the New Testament through speed reading for the first time. A young man in his early 30s promised to give 'God's comfort' and succeeded greatly. I could not even imagine what kind of person he was to be so wise. I managed to understand the book though it might be shallow. But I could not understand "No one comes to the Father except through me." From then on, I was deeply obsessed with him. Who really is Jesus?

I wrote earlier that as soon as I saw the 'Advocate' part in John 14-16 of the English Bible, I immediately concluded that it was me. Because, the primary meaning of this word is not only 'lawyer', but also it was obvious that God sent me to be the 'lawyer' and ordered me to 'pursue the truth'. Jesus describes Him as 'the Spirit of Truth' who leads to all truth. His mission is to re-disclose the identity of Jesus, and what Jesus always emphasized, and to define 'justice and sin, and judgment of god', and to inform what will happen in the future.

'He will be with you always (14:16)', 'He will teach you all things and remind you of everything that I have told you (14:26)', 'I will send to you from the Father and he will testify on my behalf (15:26)', 'When he comes, he will convict the world of sin, righteousness, and judgment (16:8)', 'He'll guide you into all truth. He won't speak on his own accord, but he'll speak whatever he hears and will declare to you the things that are to come (16:13)', 'He will glorify me, because he will take what is mine and declare it to you. (16:14-15)', etc.

Jesus also introduces the Holy Spirit as an advocate when the disciples are persecuted for believing in Jesus (Mark 13:11, Luke 12:11-12). Even after the resurrection, he told the disciples to wait (receive) the Holy Spirit (Luke 24:49, John 20:22), and if people verbally disobeyed Jesus, they would be forgiven, but if they blasphemed the "Holy Spirit," they would not be forgiven (Matthew 12:31, Luke 12:10). It seems that this Holy Spirit was very important to Jesus. Why? Why is that so?

Jesus concluded his life by saying, "I came into the world for this: to testify to the truth (John 18:37)". He said, "God is spirit, and those who worship him must worship in spirit and truth (John 4:24)". He explained about spirit, "What is born of the Spirit is spirit (John 3:6)" but there is one more beside spirit: truth. I think this 'truth' is the most important contribution of Jesus. For Him, serving God, the Spirit, must come with truth. What is the truth of Jesus?

Earlier, I said that 'even God evolves'. How does God evolve? It evolves through the interpretation of people living in a particular era. Like Abraham, who introduced the only God that exists in the mind without a form, not a statue that can be commonly encountered around.

Jesus, gifted with great intellectual sensibility, immediately recognized that the Roman Empire was the beginning of a great and irreversible civilization. The wheels of the Empire were so ruthless that the independence of the small Jewish people was not even an occasion to discuss. The subjects of the Empire have no choice but to live a life of slaves swayed by those in power. Where can humans find solace in these times? How about the god who is the friend of humans and the parent who wipes away our tears; the personal god whom we can meet anywhere, anytime, out of the temple?

The amazing thing about Jesus is that he is extremely intelligent and at the same time full of compassion for all people. It is never easy to extract a warm god who completely cares for humans from a god who reigns over humans and demands obedience. This is possible only with the extremely intelligent and extremely warm personality of

Jesus. Although this was the demand of the times, the Jewish priests did not see through it at all. If the law does not have the flexibility to meet the needs of the times, it is nothing more than a snare that ensnares people. Jesus is full of rage from the moment he appears.

To say that the splendid temple of Jerusalem will be demolished is a call to meet the demands of the new era right away. It is not a betrayal of the nation, but an expression of disappointment and frustration. It is also like saying that you cannot even read how far the momentum of the Roman Empire will reach. From the very beginning, the Jesus' grand ideal was so high, so wide, so deep that it inevitably flowed beyond Judea to all nations for thousands of years.

While his calling was ultra-modern and revolutionary, the time given to him was too short. This is why his resolution and executive power were not common. It was enough for Him to live like a flame for only 3 years, and this is why it affects us so far.

So, the God Jesus introduced to us was not the God of the Old Testament. It is a completely new God discovered by Jesus. He reinterpreted the monotheistic God of the Jewish race as his own ultra-modern God. And that God is a God that even the Old Testament God would be proud of because he had the personality of Jesus who was "strong and delicate". That is why "No one comes to the Father except through me." Why should people come to the Father (God)? On the one hand, He started out as the God of the Old Testament. On the other hand, it is because he is so wise and so humble. "If you ask me anything in my name, I will do it (John 14:14)". Although Jesus attained divinity, He still admits that He is only a human being. As far as I know, this is the 'truth' of Jesus.

It seems that Jesus foresaw that one day there would be serious challenges to himself and to those who believed in him. So, the Holy Spirit of Jesus must inevitably be the Spirit of Truth who will guide you into all truth (John 14:17, Spirit of Truth John 16:13). The lawyer He sends must act as the Spirit of the Truth.

As the Spirit of the Truth and the lawyer of Jesus, I have finally stood before mankind, so I must do my part. And I would like to start with more talks about Jesus. Jesus is the pride of Sapiens. I think we are able to know what kind of existence we really are from Jesus. We who live in language know well what kind of existence God is. Does not Jesus just fit there? He became a God among Sapiens, the pinnacle of evolution. Is not evolution then complete? I believe that the point at which Jesus acquired divinity was before the beginning of his public life. If you look at the 40 days of the wilderness trial with the devil, you can see how accurately he understands God. Looking at what Jesus did in later work, it is needless to say. The history of Christianity is inevitable, but it is unknown whether they have captured the essence of Jesus as it is.

Why did Jesus become a god? What is God's role? Is he forcibly elevating humans to divine beings? What good is a god if he cannot come to a man who moans in pain and wipes away his tears? A perfect man has no need of God. God does not condemn the original sin of weak man, that is, the animal nature, but acknowledges it as the human condition. That is the truth that Jesus so emphasized. What is truth? It is a crown of thorns. Even if you get splinters, you have to wear the crown. Jesus hung out with sinners and did not want to neglect a single one. He, of course, never judged or condemned anyone either.

Jesus loves us so much. I didn't come to condemn the world, but to save it (John 12:47). The sick need a doctor (Matthew 9:12). I did not come to call righteous people, but sinners (Mark 2:17). You have not chosen me, but I have chosen you (John 15:16). Heaven and earth will disappear, but my words will never disappear (Mark 13:31). I am with you each and every day until the end of the age (Matthew 28:20). Even that was not enough, so he promised, I'm not going to forsake you like orphans. I will come back to you (John 14:18)'.

When will Jesus return? It is right now. If we look at the signs that Jesus gave about the last day of His return, we can see how concerned Jesus was about the prevalence of atheism and the persecution of the weak. (Matthew 24, Mark 13, Luke 17 and 21) The specific time of the Second Coming is set as 'a time when women suffer horribly because their right to abortion is violated'. Do you remember what Jesus said to the women of Jerusalem at the beginning of Chapter 1 of this book? Not only does the end times begin with 'birth pains', but it also mentioned that 'how dreadful it will be for pregnant women and nursing mothers'.

Jesus also knew that there would be terrible persecution of sexual minorities. On that day, those who were on the housetop were not to go down to take anything out of the house, and those who were in the fields were not to get their cloaks. This is a declaration that they, who are not treated as members of the society and family because they are sexual minorities, are not at all lacking in the glory of the Second

Coming of Christ 'as they are on the housetop' and 'as they are in the clothes they are currently wearing.'

Jesus warns that this is a great distress that has unequaled from the beginning of the world until now and never to be equaled again. The fact that those who believe in Christ and not anyone else persecute the socially disadvantaged shows how seriously Jesus takes this. In the end, Jesus promised to 'cut short the days for the chosen ones' by returning 'at a time other than winter, that is, before it gets even more tragic'. He said that if it had not been shortened, no one would have been survived.

Jesus was most concerned about the devastation of humanity as a result of the death sentence on God, and all of this is the consequence. It is warned that Jerusalem will be surrounded by armies, will be thrown down without a single stone left on another, or will be trampled on by the Gentiles, and this is exactly what it is. Jesus then call on the Jews not to get caught in the desolation 'by warning them to flee to the mountains or not to enter the city'.

However, Jesus promised clear redemption to those who believe, saying, "You will be hated by everyone for my name's sake, and wickedness will increase, and the love of most will grow cold, but whoever stands firm to the end will not perish even a hair of the head." Jesus also knew that faith was originally a matter of individual conscience. Jesus promised to give a testimony that would shatter atheism, 'through the Holy Spirit, He will give words and wisdom that none of the adversaries will be able to resist or contradict.' Isn't that what I, Jesus' lawyer as His representative, am doing now?

Jesus affirms God's final and unequivocal victory, saying that all the people of the earth will mourn when they see the Son of Man coming on the clouds of heaven, with great power and glory. Jesus said, 'Keep watch,' and that it could be at any time, but that all the nations of the earth would know the news. Returning on the clouds means that with the help of satellites, the news of Jesus' Second Coming spreads across the entire earth in an instant. The saying, 'As lightning that comes from the east is visible even in the west, so will be the coming of Son of Man', seems to be a metaphor for my involvement as an Asian with the nickname 'Ms. Lightning'. Since I was young, I have crammed almost everything, even writing books. In Korea, we call cramming 'lightning'.

Now! Can you see the power and glory of Jesus? It is said that the sun will be darkened, moon will not give its light, and stars will fall from the sky, and heavenly bodies will be shaken, with the return of Jesus, the last God who will be with us forever. This is His prophecy that all old things, such as atheism, Darwinism, creationism, incarnation theory, and Trinity theory, will collapse immediately. Jesus' innovation was so outstanding that it had to be achieved in aspects appropriate to each era by dividing it into the First and Second Comings.

Jesus also, as a Jew, truly wishes to return home and reconcile with all religions, including Judaism. Jesus was so obsessed with His mission as the Messiah that He did not compromise with the older generation, and as a result, He succeeded greatly in creating an ultra-modern universal religion from Judaism. However, now that Jesus has returned after being caught up in the great wave of atheism, He is trying to examine His origins. Jesus desires not only the eternal restoration of the Temple of Jerusalem, the home of His Father God, but also the harmonious coexistence of all religions. That's what 'it means to know that summer is near when the leaves of the fig tree and other trees begin to sprout.'

How did Jesus anticipated all of this 2,000 years ago? Is not this truly marvelous? Are not gods and religion the ultimate adaptations of Sapiens? How is this not science? The creatures like us who live off the land live in fellowship with the holy God! Did scientists and intellectuals really win? Would Jesus have applauded those who persecute others while being religious? Since Jesus has returned to us at this time, who would He go to first?

I declare that 'God's justice is Lamarckism and sin is Darwinism, and judgment will be made accordingly'. According to Lamarckism, all multicellular organisms evolve independently, and therefore, I declare that everything that happens to a woman's body is only the woman's right to decide independently without any external interference. I also declare that LGBTQ+ are biologically perfect members of the human species. The Commandments of Jesus are to worship God of a true friend of man, and to love one another. Cannot you guess why God chooses Lamarckism, that puts peaceful coexistence, and the survival above all else, and walk together?

...

# 16

# What is Macron's role?

Lamarckism or Darwinism? France and Britain have a history of fighting for nearly 100 years over their national pride as the powerhouse in science. In the 1930s and 1940s, scientists around the world held several meetings, and sided with Darwin. What if Lamarck was eventually proven right? Is not that daughter's prophecy? I do not know how to reach the French people, but if only I could! In fact, I did a couple of things in December 2021 in the hope of attracting the attention of France. PowerKorea, a magazine sent to numerous diplomatic missions in Korea, published my interview about my scientific findings. and I also sent the scientific discovery report to a number of domestic life science journals and societies as well as the French Embassy and the French School in Seoul. But Lamarck was a man too long ago.

Though my findings are of tremendous importance, I can guess that gaining one's recognition in the scientific circles will be as challenging as picking a star in the sky. How can I claim that 'God is a scientific being, and creationism also has a great adaptive function'! Darwin is a divine being in the biological world. So If a scientist becomes a Christian, he will get a glare from his fellow scientists. Besides, I am an amateur. Christians expressed great disapproval of my advocacy for abortion and LGBTI. That was not all: biology is currently the most advanced field, and its scope is wide but it is mainly led by the West, especially the United States and the United Kingdom. With due respect to South Korea, I do not know whether it is possible that the East challeges the West with a different view. In the end, I have come to a conclusion that I myself make the way to the West.

As soon as I learned that an abortion case was pending in the U.S. Supreme Court in early January 2022, it was clear to me that I was called to the task. In May, I sent an e-mail to the Guttmacher Institute, an abortion support organization, saying, "I can help as a messenger of God." But I got no answer. My friends advised me not to mention God, saying,

'What kind of god is science?', but I had a different opinion. In terms of importance, God was 99%, and discovery was just a premise for talking about God. I was about to run to America, but Jesus stopped me, saying, "Are you in a hurry? Or Are they in a hurry? Who is more? The evil is yet to be tasted." Then, at the end of June, what finally supposed to happen happened.

When I was about to send a letter to the French Embassy Seoul, Jesus also encouraged me by saying "Cherish this opportunity very much.", and I felt hope. While studying France, I came to understand why France was chosen. The French Revolution in 1789! A country where commoners dried up the seed of nobility and eliminated the reigning king forever! Modern democracy began with the motto: Liberty, equality and fraternity. President Macron is reflecting the spirit of the French Revolution into everyday politics! 'France has a will, a cosmic aspiration to benefit the whole world.' These are the words from President Macron's book <Emmanuel Macron Revolution>. I could not stop thinking, 'God truly loves the people and leaders who love the truth!' Lamarck was the citizen of the country!

Lamarck is the founder of biology, and of the theory of evolution. While classifying invertebrate fossils, he deduced 'simultaneous evolution of males and females due to the use and disuse of organs'. However, 'Georges Cuvier', who founded paleontology while studying fossils of vertebrates, opposed Lamarck's theory, arguing for 'intelligent design theory' or 'catastrophism theory' for the reason that 'there are no intermediate organisms in the course of evolution'. Lamarck was never recognized during his lifetime. The second daughter, who took care of her father, said, "Posterity will admire you; It will avenge you, my Father." At Lamarck's funeral, when Cuvier in his speech, said "Lamarck is wrong, and I am right," the daughter stood up and fiercely criticized Cuvier, promising that "Someday it will surely be revealed that my father was right." Ever since knowing this, my nickname became 'Lamarck's daughter', because I told my sons about this everyday.

I had to honestly write why an amateur biologist from a distant country wanted to reach President Macron. When the verdict severely violated the abortion rights of American women, President Macron immediately expressed regret over the verdict, and solidarity with American women. In this situation, I wrote, "The only person who can actually help American women is President Macron, and the way is through a paradigm shift to Lamarckism." France, which gave the United States the 'Statue of Liberty' in 1886, now has the duty to present 'freedom as a substantive right'! And the method is to announce my findings to the general public so that they can judge the consistency of scientific findings. As far as I know, my findings are easy and simple.

Science is a field where 'a finding' and 'a recognition' are dealt as a different matter. In other words, recognition is as difficult as finding. For example, the theory of symbiosis, the origin of eukaryotes, was first put forward by a Russian in 1905, but there was no trace of it until an American female biologist, Lynn Margulis, introduced it to the academic world in the mid-1960s. 'Barbara McClintock', who revealed the 'jumping genes' through corn research, was also recognized after 30 years. Even if I have found such a grandiose discovery 'the origin of sex and females and males', it will be almost impossible for me to get into the academia since I am an amateur biologist from the East. But I knew that could at least help the American women, so I had to make the most of it.

Lamarck is dead already, but he is the founder of biology. So President Macron should rather restore his honor! The power to properly understand the society comes from a right paradigm. The reason religious people and scientists have been fighting for a long time, and everyone insists on their own rights is because of Darwinism which sees the world as a field of competition for survival. We should no longer let this old and wrong Darwinism rule the world. Lamarckism is a theory of peaceful coexistence that survival is achieved not through competition but through mutual respect and cooperation. Are not people anxious about the climate crisis, earthquakes and wars? Is not France the country where the people of Esprit live and accept the truth most quickly? People of Esprit! Open a new era and receive great rewards (e.g., Nobel Peace Prize)! France cannot refuse a man who hears the voice of God! Is not France the country of Joan of Arc who saved her country by listening to the voice of God? I, too, heard the voice of God and came here!

Was it because it was too grandiose? There was no response at all. There are so many difficult matters going on within the Korean Bar Association, and I wanted to help even in an absurd way to be recognized in the world as 'God's lawyer'. But everything I did was a complete failure! Nevertheless, disappointment and frustration are not a sign of God's lawyer! Although there was a delay in the recognition of my discovery, I have accumulated a deep understanding about the true meaning of my discovery in return. I started writing a book at the end of November, but Jesus had a different idea at this time too: He vehemently asked me to prepare for the Second Coming of Christ! And it has come to this far.

What would be the most surprising thing to returned Jesus who was a realistic idealist and revolutionary and who devoted his whole life to nothing but 'truth'? After seeing the huge and ruthless Roman Empire, He introduced the almighty God who would exchange intimate friendships out of concern for those who would become fragments of power! In the era of advanced civilization, religion offers people consolation from painful reality as well as independence from ruthless politics. Religion, which soothes the fatigue of people's adaptation in the political realm, requires a certain balance between politics and mutual inviolability. Therefore, although the separation of church and state is inherently essential, it was too premature in the time of Jesus, and in the end Jesus lost his life like a flower. It seems that Jesus did not know that religion would dominate politics for so long. Is not this great irony? This only shows the excellent wisdom of Jesus.

Could Jesus have conceived of the existence of French people who realized their righteous anger to the limit against the corrupt and reigning power? When we look at the Bible passages about the Second Coming of Jesus, surprisingly,

Jesus knows everything that will happen after his death until modern times. I think He would smile right away with pride the moment He met the French above, and might say, "You are indeed my disciples!" Did not Jesus also say, when He spreads His will, those with the same mind as Him are His parents but not His birth parents? Didn't He insist on a disciple's determination to refuse even his father's funeral? What worthwhile thing can be achieved without that much rigor?

Jesus objected to divorce because it meant hell for women at that time. Is there anyone else who is full of love for the weak like Jesus? Is not it the true spirit of religion to be more considerate of the weak? Although feminism today still has a long way to go, it seems Jesus would be delighted to see women's status improved this much. As a result, he called me, a woman, as his representative and entrusted me with the task of 'exodus of all living things, including women and sexual minorities.' Last year, 40 years after Jesus appeared before my eyes in the resurrected form and gave me the duty to pursue the truth when I was a freshman in college, my public ministry began with the resolution of the issue of women's abortion rights. In this way, Jesus blessed true equality and reconciliation between men and women.

How did Jesus invite women to this big event in the male-dominant history? The mysteries and wonders of Jesus are beyond embroidery. Have you ever witnessed such a wise man? Have you ever seen a person who fulfills the promise he made when he passed away after 2000 years later?

Jesus, who was crucified by the tyrant Pontius Pilate, would be most happy to see a powerful person like Macron, even if it is not for personal reasons. Didn't Jesus already foresee the civilizational and social development of mankind at the time of his life and create a universal religion, assuming that individuals would be alienated by those in power or the political system? As a result, Jesus would feel proud to see today's democratic nation where everyone is equal and technology is advanced. And there are righteous and wise political leaders at the pinnacle of this progress. Macron, who pursues the well-being of the Earth, the cradle of all life, the preservation of biodiversity, and peace for all sapiens, must be the love of Jesus. Is not it amazing that the spirit of the French Revolution, the spirit of Lamarckism, and the spirit of Jesus, that is, the spirit of prioritizing mutual peaceful coexistence and individual dignity, all have in common? So, is there someone else other than Macron as the representative who will welcome Jesus who returns forever to our side? The 21st century should be the time for leaders like Macron. Since it started with the purpose of reaching Macron from the beginning, the credit for realizing the contents of this book belongs to Macron.

Why does Jesus return now? What is the true meaning of Jesus' second coming? Life, which was born by chance 3.8 billion years ago, began evolving to continue that life, and finally reached its peak in Jesus. Isn't God evolution? The 'Tree of Life' that appears at the beginning of the Old Testament and the end of the New Testament can be said to be 'the very Tree of Life' mentioned by Lamarck and Darwin, pioneers of science. In other words, evolution was the truth, the way, and the life! This is the path that the human Jesus walked, and this is the path that we take to reach the wonderful God, Jesus!

After Adam and Eve acquired the ability to discern between good and evil through the fruit of the tree of good and evil, they were expelled from paradise for fear of gaining eternal life through the fruit of the tree of life. In other words, as language evolved as a tool for thinking and began to distinguish between good and evil, people were driven out for fear of becoming like gods through knowledge. However, Jesus plunged headlong into the world of full-fledged truth pursuit, acquired divinity for himself, and gained eternal life. And he invited all mankind to the path he took first. Human knowledge, which was considered fearful, came to Jesus and saved humanity.

The Revelation prophesies that 'I saw a new heaven and a new earth, the first heaven and the first earth had passed away', and that 'God will dwell with His people and will wipe every tear from their eyes, and there will be no more death.' The One seated on the throne promises, 'It is done,' and 'I am the Alpha and the Omega, and I will give freely from the spring of the water of life to the thirsty.' (Revelation 21:1-6) In the middle of New Jerusalem, the river with the water of life flows from the throne of God and the Christ, and on each side of the river grows the tree of life, which bears twelve crops of fruit every month, and whose leaves heal the nations (Revelation 2:1-2).

The returned Jesus shows that man and God are not two bodies, but that divinity is the ultimate of humanity. Jesus declared that God is the God of all living people, and this is quite natural. Jesus, who returned by Lamarck, truly opens the kingdom of God on earth and the lost paradise is restored. All living things will coexist peacefully in their ecological niche, humans will also achieve harmony between men and women, East and West, religion and science, and religious pluralism will be achieved among all religions. The Second Coming of Jesus is humanity's greatest science festival!

# Epilogue

'First of all, you must know that it is about my power and glory as the God. Secondly, you should know that this award is given to you because you have done well in your duty to seek the truth as My lawyer. This is a matter of the authority of the God, and strictly speaking, you are not the one who gives them.'

On August 8, 2022, heavy rain flooded Gangnam and Gyodae stations. So I parked my car in the parking lot of the Korean Bar Association Hall and walked home. I thought of Jesus and filled with emotion by His grace and could not stop crying all the way. I got home and I was washing my hands when I heard the voice of Jesus saying, "If the (Jerusalem) temple is demolished, I said I would build it in three days, but since the house of lawyers is the temple, I will actually raise a building for the Korean Bar Association." I was taken aback by this sudden voice of Jesus and posted it on the executive group chat room of the association. The Korean Bar Association does not yet have its own building.

According to Lamarck's theory of evolution, God is the supreme scientific phenomenon. So I have nothing to hold back from hearing the voice of God, and explained it number of times in the chat room so that they do not take me odd but normal as before. I had this feeling that He would build a magnificent public building to reveal the glory and power of God.

However, I eventually canceled it. The reason was trivial. When I came as vice president for a one-year term, the executives posted congratulation comments in the chat room whenever a member's birthday turns up. And it was so good because it looked to me a sign that I surely belong to them as a member even though there was no party or gifts. But no one congratulated me on my birthday.

Then and now, I am very proud of myself as 'God's lawyer'

because without it, I could never dare to do what I am doing now. By nightfall, I was terribly wounded. "God's lawyer? Ridiculous! There's no place here for such a weirdo like you!" I felt as if they were saying this to me, and I felt rejected. If 'someone' says this is not something to be disappointed, I have nothing to say. But then why was I so hurt at that time? Because, I pondered, my pride of being the blessed lawyer sent here (KBA) was hurt. About a week later, I posted again declaring, 'I withdraw the blessing given to the association considering the current circumstances'. I felt a bit relieved afterwards.

But that became another task for me, the God's lawyer. The question was whether humans could reject the voice of God. There was no reproof from the God for withdrawing the voice of Him but I had to suffer quite a while. I sought for an answer but there was none, and I put it aside thinking He will say again His true will (about this) in time.

This book was written suddenly from January 21, and a few days ago, Jesus brought out the matter for the association building again. After asking and receiving numerous questions to and from Jesus, I finally obtained the answer for the bullet points, and thought it would be good to be included in this book, and was decided so. It is not like I am dictating the words of Jesus one by one, but because he throws me questions with a big sound of resonance, there is no way I can skip them without solving. So I wrote them here, but I absolutely have no idea what He will do or how He will do. In this regard, my feelings right now can be considered vaguely the same as when I finished the book in 2021, that 'I was in charge of the Second Coming of Jesus, and of integrating religion and science'. I actually do not know either. I just took the command and wrote it down.

When I started to serve as the vice president of the association, a generational shift from the old (Judicial exam) to the new (bar exam) lawyers was in progress. How different the new ones from the old ones like me! And keeping their lawyer's job was the main issue on the talk table due to the overflowing number of bar-exam passers while the market demand is decreasing alongside the population and the number of cases they usually get. I, who viewed the concept of ecological status as a profession in the human world, fully sympathized with their view of the world, and I always supported them. They worked as if they were fighting a war, since they were perpetually infiltrated the unique area of attorney practice from adjacent professions, they always had to defend themselves. I thought they had to do this because seniors like me have not done our homework on time. I felt sorry for their excessive efforts. And I regretted the fact that the Darwinism's 'live-race' is ruling the world. If it would have been the Lamarckism's peaceful symbiotic world view, a point of mutual immobility between professions could be made.

If occasion arises, I would like to express my gratitude to the 51st executives and staff members of the Korean Bar Association, including President Lee Jong-yop. I, who had no intention of becoming a lawyer, would be the most unsuitable executive. How absurd I must have been to make such a fuss about getting recognition for my scientific discovery, saying that I was now defending God, not man? I am just so grateful that no one of them blamed me but treated me nicely. I wish the association tremendous success and bright future for everyone. For the time being, I hope the keeping their job issue will be solved through policy revision so that they can save their unnecessary energy wasted over the worries rather than defending their clients at the court.

**

Now I have to write down the reason why there are no reference books even though this is a science book. In my first book, which revealed the evolution of sex, there were 400 books for reference. I had just made a scientific discovery then, so I should have read all those books. But since this book aims at the recognition of my scientific discoveries, I feel to say that I have a little more room than then? This book attempts to integrate science and religion. And the reason for that was, according to Lamarck's theory of evolution, religion became a scientific phenomenon, so it was possible to discuss it largely within the framework of science.

All of the life history of living things written in this book is at the level of scientific common sense found in life science textbooks. Since I used my own analytical framework of 'the inheritance of life history' to analyze and systematize the basic life history of prokaryotes, protists and multicellular organisms, scientists should not feel difficult to judge the scientific nature and the new discoveries written on this book without references. How fortunate I am not to have to cite the unique experiments of unknown scientists.

In addition, regarding the divinity of the God Jesus written in this book, I make it clear here that the actions of Jesus recorded in the 4 Gospels of the New Testament were extracted and analyzed by the paradigm of Lamarck's theory of evolution. If you think what I have explained in this book is underdeveloped or if you want to know the reference books that I have read, please refer to my first book.

In relation to American women, President Macron and President Biden, the Korean Bar Association, collective nouns or human lives that appeared in the title or epilogue of this book, I would like to make an excuse that I had no desire to unfairly use or cause trouble for selfish purposes. I used them because my scientific discovery has not yet been recognized by the scientific world, and I wrote the above names for the purpose of recognition but nothing more. I will take the accusation if people think I rather used them and my discoveries have not yet been acknowledged, but then I will cite the Words of Jesus Christ. For me, just as the fellowship between Jesus Christ and Jehovah God was the truth, the fellowship between me and Jesus Christ is also the truth. And as far as I know, my scientific findings are also true.

**

This book came out suddenly with an unplanned content and format. I said to myself, 'Can a book come out so suddenly like this?' Moreover, it is a book in Korean-English translation! I could not help but feeling books also have their destiny. The idea of English translation of my book came about when I accidentally tried the Google Translate app. As I got used to it, the speed increased. Then, I needed someone to do the final touch. And I remembered PowerKorea reporter John Kim who did the English translation without hesitation when I published my scientific interview on the magazine. I asked him, and he, as well as the chief editor of the magazine, gladly said OK with the offer. It was written in a hurry, sent chapter by chapter, and John touched it and sent it back to me with such a speed. I am so thankful for him.

As for the design, I contacted Lim Yu-jin who designed my first book two years ago. She has this excellent sense to read my intentions and reflects them in the design even though it was a science book. Then and now, things rolled in a hurry as if it were a guerrilla war. And I am just so grateful that she followed my lead with a great outcome. I also express my gratitude to my husband Kwang-seup and my two sons Kyu-tae and Kyu-ho. It must have been uneasy for them to see a family member preoccupied with something that no one knew about for almost 7 years. I am very grateful to them for leaving me alone.

# American version epilogue

Whoever has ears, let them hear what the Spirit says to the churches. To the one who is victorious, I will give the right to eat from the tree of life, which is in the paradise of God.

Revelation 2:7 NIV

I know your afflictions and your poverty—yet you are rich! I know about the slander of those who say they are Jews and are not, but are a synagogue of Satan.

Revelation 2:9 NIV

So he returned home to his father. And while he was still a long way off, his father saw him coming. Filled with love and compassion, he ran to his son, embraced him, and kissed him.

Luke 15:20 NLT

"You will not certainly die," the serpent said to the woman.

Genesis 3:4 NIV

The Lord will mediate between nations and will settle international disputes. They will hammer their swords into plowshares and their spears into pruning hooks. Nation will no longer fight against nation, nor train for war anymore.

Isaiah 2:4 NLT

Title

**The Mechanism of the Evolution of Sex, a New Evolutional Theory: The Use and Disuse of Organs according to the Principle of the Precedence of Survival over Reproduction, the Report of Scientific Discoveries including the Brain-Based Personality Type Hypothesis (and the Request for the Evaluation of Scientific Validity of Scientific Discoveries )**

**To**

1. The Microbiological Society of Korea (president: Jung-Yun Kim)
   Rm. 810, Korea Science and Technology Center (KSTC) New Building, 22, Teheran-ro 7-gil, Gangnam-gu, Seoul (T.3453-3321)
2. The Korean Society for Microbiology (president: Jun-Haeng Lee)
   Rm. 701, Korea Science and Technology Center (KSTC) New Building, 22, Teheran-ro 7-gil, Gangnam-gu, Seoul (T.887-3062)
3. The Korean Society of Protistologists (president: Young-Ok Kim)

The Korea Institute of Ocean Science & Technology, 385, Haeyang-ro, Yeongdo-gu, Busan (T.051-664-3000)

4. The Korean Society of Phycology (president: Myung-Suk Kim)

   Rm. 1716, International Trade Center Building A, 72, Iljik-ro, Gwangmyeong-si, Gyeonggi-do (T.899-5980)

5. The Korean Society of Mycology (president: Hyang-Bum Lee)

   Rm. 427, Korea University College of Life Science & Biotechnology - West Building, 145, Anam-ro, Seongbuk-gu, Seoul (T.953-8355)

6. The Korean Society for Integrative Biology (president: Chang-Jong Lee)

   Rm. 1002, Korea Science and Technology Center (KSTC) New Building, 22, Teheran-ro 7-gil, Gangnam-gu, Seoul (T.554-8803)

7. The Ecological Society of Korea (president: Hun-Bok Lee)

   Rm. 104, Korea Environmental Industry and Technology Institute (KEITI) Bd. B, 215, Jinheung-ro, Eunpyeong-gu, Seoul

8. The Korean Society of Systematic Zoology (president: Gi-Sik Min)

Rm, 1002, Korea Science & Technology Federation Center, 635-4, Yeoksam-dong, Gangnam-gu, Seoul (T.569-0133)

9. The Korean Society of Plant Taxonomists (president: Jin-Oh Hyun)

2F, Korea National Arboretum, KH, 415, Gwangneungsumogwon-ro, Soheul-eup, Pocheon-si, Gyeonggi-do (T.031-543-1968)

10. The Korean Society of Plant Biologists (president: Nam-Cheon Baek)

Rm. 402, Keumsung Building, 295-1, Bongcheon-ro, Gwanak-gu, Seoul (T.884-0384)

11. The Entomological Society of Korea (president: Yeon-Su Han)

The Korean Entomological Institute, Korea University, 145, Anam-ro, Seongbuk-gu, Seoul (T.3290-3813)

12. The Ichthyological Society of Korea (presient: Jong-Young Park)

The Department of Biological Sciences, College of Natural Science, Jeonbuk National University, 567, Baekje-daero, Deokjin-gu, Jeonju-si, Jeollabuk-do

13. The Korean Research Society of Herpetologists (president: Sang-Chul Lee)

(Research Center for Endangered Species) 23, Gowal-gil,

Yeongyang-eup, Yeongyang-gun, Gyeongsangbuk-do
(T.054-680-7230)

14. The Korean Society of Phycology (president: Hee-Young
    Chae)
    Office of the Korean Society of Phycology, Bd. C, 62-12,
    Techno 1-ro, Yuseong-gu, Daejeon (H.010-4107-7980)

15. The Korean Psychological Association (president: Eun-
    Jin Jang)
    Rm. 906, Seoul Forest Halla Eco Valley, Ttukseom-ro 1-gil,
    Seongdong-gu, Seoul (T.567-0102)

16. The Korean Social and Personality Psychological
    Association (president: Hun-Seok Choi)
    Department of Psychology, College of Social Sciences,
    Sungkyunkwan University, 25-2, Seonggyungwan-ro,
    Jongno-gu, Seoul (T.760-1280)

17. The Korean Society for Cognitive and Biological
    Psychology (president: Yang-Seok Cho)
    Rm. B102, Uncho-Useoun Hall, 145, Anam-ro, Seongbuk-gu,
    Seoul (T.070-7807-2324)

18. The National Research Foundation of Korea (president:
    Kwang-Bok Lee)
    25, Heolleung-ro, Seocho-gu, Seoul (T.3460-5500)

19. The National Institute of Ecology (president: Do-Sun Jo)

1210, Geumgang-ro, Maseo-myeon, Seocheon-gun, Chungcheongnam-do (T.041-950-5300)

20. The Korea National Arboretum (president: Young-Tae Choi)

509, Gwangneungsumogwon-ro, Soheul-eup, Pocheon-si, Gyeonggi-do (T.031-540-2000)

21. The Korea Institute of Ocean Science & Technology (KIOST) (president: Woong-Seo Kim)

385, Haeyang-ro, Yeongdo-gu, Busan (T.051-664-3000)

22. Minister of Science and ICT, Jong-ho Lee

194, Gareum-ro, Sejong-si

23. Donga Scienc (representaive: Kyung-Ae Jang)

7F, 109, Cheongpa-ro, Yongsan-gu, Seoul, (T.6749-2000)

24. Science Donga (editor-in-chief: Hyun-kyung Lee)

7F, 109, Cheongpa-ro, Yongsan-gu, Seoul (T.6749-2000)

25. The Embassy of France in Korea (ambassador: Philippe Lefort))

18F, Woori Building 42, Chilpae-ro, Jung-gu, Seoul, (T.3149-4300)

26. The French School of Seoul Lycée français de Séoul (LFS) (head teacher: Hirm-Martin Bruno; teachers: Bouttemy Franck, Ochs Matthieu)

7, Seorae-ro, Seocho-gu, Seoul (T.535-1158)

27. The Embassy of Japan in Korea (embassador: Aiboshi
   Koichi)
   Twin Tree Tower A, 6, Yulgok-ro 4-gil, Jongno-gu, Seoul
   (T.2170-5200)
28. The U.S. Embassy in Korea (deputy chief of mission
   (DCM): Christopher Del Corso)
   188, Sejong-daero, Jongno-gu, Seoul (T.397-4114)
29. The Embassy of Germany in Korea (ambassador: Michael
   Reiffenstuel)
   416 8F, 416, Hangang-daero, Jung-gu, Seoul (T.748-4114)
30. British Embassy Seoul (embassador: Simon Smith)
   Sejong-daero 19-gil, Jung-gu, Seoul (T.3210-5500)

**From**

Sung-Hee Kwon (lawyer, amateur scientist)

Rm. 803, Lawfirm Tower, 25, Seocho-daero 51-gil, Seocho-gu,
   Seoul

**CC**

1. Journalists of Korean new media and news agencies
2. Foreign correspondents and journalists from foreign
   media and international new agencies in Korea

**This letter was mailed on December 22, 2021.**

## 1. Greeting and Introduction

First, I hope this letter finds you in good health, and I also wish you continued happiness, and prosperity. I am very sorry to bother you and take up your valuable time with this letter, but I would greatly appreciate it if you would kindly spare some time to read this letter.

I am a divorce lawyer working in Korea and an amateur scientist. I have recently published a science book titled *The Evolution of Sex Through the Inheritance of Life History and Speciation as a Result of the Use and Disuse of Organs* (publisher: Evolution and Mankind; publication date: August 20, 2021; legal deposit date (the National Library of Korea): August 30, 2021), This book deals with the topics described in the above title of this letter.

Since the contents of this book include new discoveries in biology, I mailed a free copy to about 200 people in order to introduce my book when this book started to be sold at online bookstores. I have also been promoting this book through a number of monthly magazine since mid-October, 2021. Because the news about my book should reach the scientific community, I mailed a free copy to science journalists of daily newspapers, publishers of magazines on science, and some renowned people in the field of science.

However, my book has received little attention probably because I am not a professional scientist. Thus, I decided to write this letter after long consideration. Some people advised me to submit a summary of the contents of the book to international scientific journals, but I think it is rather inappropriate to republish the contents of a book deposited with the National Library of Korea.

I'd like to give you an explanation about the long recipient list of this letter. Academic societies in biological fields are institutions that have the authority to receive and evaluate reports on the ecology of organisms, which is related to my findings and served as the background of my research. Since I couldn't determine which societies are more relevant to my findings, I decided to mail this letter to all the societies in the recipient list.

I examined the evolution of organisms in terms of the inheritance of life history, so I classified organisms into the three kingdoms of prokaryotes, protists, and multicellular organisms, and biological societies have been listed according to the order of the evolution of three kinds of organisms. Three psychological societies have been included since they are scientific institutions related to my theory on brain-based personality types among my research results.

I have also included several national institutions of Korea in the recipient list because I am Korean and I have a duty to report my scientific discoveries as well as a right to receive the evaluation of my discoveries in consideration of the scientific significance of my findings. I have also included magazines about science such as Donga Science in the recipient list because they deal with scientific news. Meanwhile, you may be curious about the reason I also send this letter to five foreign countries' embassies in Korea, and I'd like to explain the reason below.

The Embassy of France in Korea represents France, the native country of Jean-Baptiste de Lamarck (hereafter, Lamarck). Lamarck proposed the evolutionary theory about the simultaneous acquisition of traits by males and females through the use and disuse of organs for the first time in the history of biology. Nevertheless, his theory and accomplishments have not yet been properly evaluated and duly recognized. The statue of Lamarck in the Garden of Plants (Jardin des Plantes) in Paris is reported to have an inscription showing his daughter's prediction that posterity would avenge his father. If the return of Lamarckism is scientifically recognized, the French people will be more delighted than anyone else. I have included the French School of Seoul (Lycée français de Séoul: LFS) in the recipient list of this letter, because I thought that two biology teachers of the school may be able to transmit their scientific opinions about my research results to the Embassy of France in Korea if necessary. If the teachers could kindly present their opinions, they would be the first scientific views on my findings.

Japan is the most powerful country in the field of evolutionary biology, and it produced globally respected biologists such as Moto Kimura and Susumu Tonegawa. Moto Kimura suggested the neutral theory of molecular evolution, and Susumu Tonegawa found the principle of antibody formation in somatic cells. I obtained a crucial insight about 'the evolution through genetic changes of somatic cells (stem cells)' from these two biologists' theories. In Japan, research on the evolution of sex has been actively conducted in recent years, so four Korean-translated books on evolution by Japanese authors have been published in Korea in the past ten years. Research on evolution has also been actively conducted in Japan. I gained great help for my research from books written by Japanese biologists such as Shinichi Fukuoka, Hidehiro Inagaki, Eisuke Hasegawa, Koichiro Fujita, and Yoshitaka Kamimura. The Newton Highlight series written by Japanese authors and published as separate volumes were also useful research material for my biological study.

With respect to the development of modern biology, we cannot but mention the notable accomplishments of American biologists. Among many American biologists, Richard Charles Lewontin, who dauntlessly criticized genetic determinism, provided invaluable guidance in my research when I found it difficult to accept Darwin's evolutionary theory and felt confused due to my lack of knowledge. I also gained confidence in new biology from the American evolutionary biologist Joan Roughgarden and the American philosopher Alvin Plantinga, Joan Roughgarden conducted research on the biology of sexual minorities, and Alvin Plantinga studied Christian philosophy, which can be called the supreme field of science. I also obtained great help from research books written by a number of American scientists, including Barbara McClintock, Temple Grandin, Stephen J. Gould, Sean B. Carroll, Paul Colinvaux, Adrian Forsyth, Robin C. Moran, Douglas Emlen, Richard Prum, Michael Ryan, Stephanie Elizabeth Mohr, and Bruce H. Lipton.

Germany is the native country of Klaus Hausmann, Norbert Hulsmann, and Renate Radek, three coauthors of the book *Protistology*, a study on protists, which are miraculous organisms in the history of evolution of living things on the planet. This book is one of the important references of my book, so it appears on the first line of the reference list. Protists are organisms that evolved sexual reproduction, and have the essential nature of all multicellular organisms. Germany is the homeland of Gerhard Roth, the author of the book *The Long Evolution of Brains and Minds*, which is the first book on evolutionary biology that I read on December 1, 2016. It is also the native country of Christiane Nüsslein-Volhard, the German biologist who studied the genome of fruit flies. In addition, this country also produced the music band Enigma, whose music had been with me throughout my intellectual wandering for five years.

Meanwhile, the U.K. is the native country of Charles Darwin, the father of modern evolutionary theory, so if my theory is recognized, it may be unwelcome news for the U.K. However, when the collapse of Darwin's Arch occurred in mid-May, it appeared to symbolize the end of life of Darwinism, so I decided to send this letter to the British Embassy Seoul as well. It is an undeniable fact that Darwin's evolutionary theory played a pivotal role in modern science and greatly contributed to the development of modern science despite the limitations of his time. Even though his theory received a disproportionate amount of attention, it is not his fault but subsequent generations of scientists are responsible for this problem.

The mechanism of the evolution of sex and the mechanism of speciation have been the biggest unsolved conundrums that all biologists around the world have been trying to solve. I feel honored to have the good fortune of finding answers to these mysteries thanks to all the previous research endeavors of numerous biologists. In other words, I was able to obtain the results of my research "by standing on the shoulders of giants" as the famous scientist Isaac Newton said. The pursuit of truth and truthfulness is the essential nature of our species Homo sapiens, and I think that this applies to all humans regardless of whether an individual is a professional, a foreigner, or a woman. I would like to implore the ambassadors of the embassies listed above to submit my scientific discovery report and the request for the evaluation of scientific validity of my findings with this letter and my book to an authoritative scientific institution in their native country on my behalf.

Finally, I'd like to tell all those concerned of the places who receive this letter that if anyone wants to meet me in person, I would gladly pay a visit and answer each question as earnestly as possible like a student taking an oral exam in school. I will also sincerely respond to every written inquiry at any time. I would be greatly honored if you could spare some time to read this letter and give sincere consideration to the contents of this letter.

## 2. Reasons for Starting My Research

Despite my job as a lawyer, I became fascinated by biology and found myself engrossed in this field of science. My fascination with biology is related to my personal history. While handling divorce cases as a lawyer, I noticed that people with opposite personality traits often get married, although personality differences are the most common reason for divorce.

When I was wondering about possible causes behind this apparently strange phenomenon, I accidentally encountered the triune brain theory, so it occurred to me that humans' personality types and the marriages of two individuals with opposite personality traits may be evolutionary phenomena. When I was faced with my divorce crisis, I managed to overcome it partly due to my clients' advice against divorce. However, in an attempt to overcome my marital problems, I started to study the evolutionary process of the human brain.

During this study, I thought that if I could understand the evolution of personality types, I might be able to overcome my long-term depression. Although I conducted this research during a relatively short period, the study helped me to overcome my marital conflicts and I also succeeded in curing my depression in a short time. Then, I came to have the desire to conduct an in-depth study on personality types as an evolutionary phenomenon in the future. In December, 2016, I was finally able to make time for my biological study and began with the evolution of the brain of animals. As a result, I summarized the evolutionary processes of the human brain. The conclusions of my research during this period are summarized below in the third section about my findings.

In the course of studying biology, I inevitably encountered Charles Darwin's evolutionary theory, and although I was a novice biology student, I found it difficult to accept this theory. However much I tried, I couldn't convince myself of the view that organisms brought about big evolutionary events such as speciation through selection by external nature rather than actively adapting to the environment.

I also found it difficult to accept the claim that the sexual dimorphism of animals such as the tail of peacocks is a result of selection by the opposite sex. Considering that all organisms survive and reproduce, it also seemed strange to me that there is no correlation between natural selection and sexual selection.

The theory of the use and disuse of organs proposed by Lamarck seemed more logical. According to Lamarck's evolutionary theory, the evolution of a species occurred as the male and female members of a species simultaneously acquired common adaptive traits for survival as a result of the use and disuse of organs due to changes in 'internal vital forces.' Anyway, it is clear that all animals found around us have two sexes and the opposite sexes live together in peace, In addition, regarding the claim that organisms evolved by using their organs due to 'internal vital forces,'

I thought that it is a natural way of existence for organisms that live as active agents in their life. In the course of my biological study, I became aware that the sexual reproduction of animals and plants is one of the greatest unresolved mysteries in biology, and it was a very interesting topic for me.

I made up my mind to delve into this biological mystery as deeply as possible, even if I couldn't find an answer. I devoted all my spare time except for the time for my daily duties to this study, and was deeply engrossed in this intellectual inquiry. I continuously read many books in the various fields of biology, including science books for students as well as more detailed science books for the general public.

As a result, I luckily stumbled upon the mechanism of sexual reproduction on January 1, 2020, and found the origin of the existence of two sexes, male and female on March 28, 2020. I immediately started to write a book on my findings, but it was a very difficult task for me. Thus, I decided to write a paper instead of a book, and finished writing an 11-page paper after working on it for one month from July, 1, 2020.

I attempted to publish my paper through an academic journal or magazine, but I couldn't find such an opportunity easily due to my limitations as an amateur biologist. Thus, I considered writing a book based on the contents of my paper, and I started to write a book on August 8, 2020.

I finished writing my explanations about the mechanism of the evolution of sex in February, 2021, but I wanted to additionally describe the mechanism of speciation through the use and disuse of organs because I, as a daughter of

Lamarck, had already constructed this theory in my mind. I finally finished the final draft of my book at the beginning of August, 2021. It was the completion of my long and arduous research conducted by perusing about 400 books on biology over a period of about five years.

**3. Contents of the Report of Scientific Discoveries (and the Request for the Evaluation of the Scientific Validity of the Discoveries)**

**A. Facts Used as Premises**

I classified organisms into the three kingdoms of prokaryotes, protists, and multicellular organisms. Protists are thought to have emerged through predation between prokaryotes as follows. When predation between prokaryotes occurred, the parasitic organisms evolved into mitochondrias and came to live together. Multicellular organisms are thought to be protists that acquired the multicellularity factor and came to live in a group.

In short, since the elements of prokaryotes are hidden in protists and multicellular organisms, when the life histories of prokaryotes are required, they are exhibited in a modified form suitable for the system of descendant organisms. In addition, because multicellular organisms are still essentially protists, they have the same life history as protists except for multicellularity. These facts are thought to be the clues that reveal the secret of evolution

In addition, all organisms primarily pursue survival, and reproduction is thought to be a method for extending survival. Therefore, 'the precedence of metabolism over replication' or 'the precedence of survival over reproduction' is the great principle that regulates the life of the organisms of three kingdoms. Chromosomes, genomes, or genes are beings for equipping the relationship between cells and the environment with the presentness of adaptation.

In particular, when multicellular organisms emerged, the interest conflict between survival and reproduction occurred. As a result, survival-related life history and reproductive life history are strictly distinguished from each other in the life of organisms, but the principle of the precedence of survival over reproduction is not violated in the mode of reproduction or reproductive behavior.

Meanwhile, all organisms live according to the principle of the exclusion of competition in order to seek stable survival, and it is the reason why each species continuously forms its ecological niche and bring about speciation. Due to the same reason, organisms set territories even within the same species, and determine ranks among individuals when living in groups.

Further, the speciation of multicellular organisms can be understood more easily from the perspective that multicellular organisms are, in essence, protists with the elements of prokaryotes. Speciation occurs primarily in a direction toward increasing the possibility of survival of individuals in the ecological niche.

However, I think that since multicellular organisms are, in essence, unicellular eukaryotes, speciation inevitably occurs at a species level. In addition, speciation seems to be materialized in a concrete form through the simultaneous evolution of male and female gametophytes through simultaneous formation of two germ cells on the one hand and the acquisition of traits by somatic cells on the other.

## B. The Mechanism of Evolution of Sex

**To see things in the seed, that is genius (Laotzu, around 600 BC)**

**Why are there two sexes? … Why did two sexes come into being? (from The Origins of Creativity by Edward Wilson)**

**The evolution of sex has emerged as the queen of evolutionary problems that have not yet been solved in the 20th century. (from Life Ascending: The Ten Great Inventions of Evolution by Nick Lane)**

## (1) Prokaryotes : The Union of Cells and Metabolites

The survival-related life history of prokaryotes includes horizontal gene transfer, endospores, and immunity, and their reproductive life history is self-replication.

## (2) Protists: Symbiosis Following Predation Between Prokaryotes

Protists include haploid trophic forms and diploid trophic forms, and it is thought that the evolution of haploid trophic forms occurred earlier. Haploid trophic forms vertically inherited the life history of prokaryotes, including the survival-related life history such as horizontal gene transfer, endospores, and immunity, and the reproductive life history such as self-replication.

Horizontal gene transfer seems to have been modified in such a way that haploid trophic forms become diploid through conjugation to endure a harsh environment in an unfavorable environment, and undergo meiosis when the environment becomes favorable again, as shown in dinoflagellate cysts. Using two modes of reproduction in this way is more favorable for survival just like it is harder to break two branches than a single branch.

Endospores seem to have been modified in such a way that protists form hard survival structures when necessary (resistant cysts of amoebas and ciliates). However, endospores seem to be frequently inherited in combination with horizontal gene transfer. Self-replication is also inherited because it is the method of replicating protists as they are regardless of the genetic arrangement.

Protists that are haploid trophic forms form reproductive cells through mitosis in an unfavorable environment, and become rigid diploid zygotes through cell fusion to endure the harsh environment. Then, when the environment becomes favorable again, they return to the original trophic forms through meiosis and reproduce by self-replication, and this is a mode of sexual reproduction.

In other words, protists evolved sexual reproduction as an innovative method for pursuing survival and reproduction simultaneously through the inheritance of a combination of the horizontal gene transfer, endospores, and self-replication of ancestors. The combination of diploid zygotes and the property of a hard survival structure is thought to be the optimal method for enduring a harsh environment.

In the process, protists added the following elements: forming germ cells through mitosis and the method of meiosis for diploid zygotes to subsequently return to the original trophic form.

On the other hand, protists also include diploid trophic forms. The evolution of these diploid trophic forms is thought to have occurred in the following way. When haploid trophic forms temporarily became diploid zygotes during the sexual reproduction process, they remained diploid for environmental causes instead of returning to the original trophic form, and eventually evolved into diploid organisms. In other words, diploid trophic forms have a pair of chromosomes, and they seem to have emerged in the movement process of organisms to a harsher environment.

Diploid protists vertically inherited the survival life history, such as endospores and immunity, and the reproductive life history of self-replication, and it seems that since their usual form was already diploid, they didn't inherit horizontal gene transfer separately as shown in dinoflagellate cysts.

Meanwhile, diploid protists evolved in the process of sexual reproduction of halploid protists, and since they were diploid, they probably had to live in an unfavorable environment in many cases and frequently reproduced by sexual reproduction. However, it is thought that because they are diploid trophic forms, they form germ cells through meiosis, they become diploid through reproductive cell fusion to endure the harsh environment, and when the environment becomes favorable again, they reproduce by mitosis.

Whether the organisms were either haploid trophic forms or diploid trophic forms, only two types of germ cells, homozygous and heterozygous germ cells, were produced simultaneously, and it is thought to be a method for preventing genetic deformities and infertility resulting from excessive combination. In fungi, which have not two sexes but multiple sexes, the conjugation of only two individuals occurs. Thus, it is thought that heterozygous germ cells evolved as a trait for ensuring fast conjugation.

## (3) Multicellular Organisms: Protists came to live in a group by acquiring the multicellularity factor

I think that multicellular organisms evolved from protists by acquiring the multicellularity factor, on the basis of the facts given below. First, in multicellular organisms, a fertilized egg repeatedly undergoes mitosis to grow into the body of a multicellular organism. In addition, each somatic cell of multicellular organisms shares the nucleus with the same chromosomes.

As to the mode of reproduction, depending on whether they are haploid or diploid, multicellular organisms form unicellular haploid germ cells through mitosis or meiosis like protists. These facts all suggest that multicellular organisms evolved from protists. In addition, I presumed that the earliest multicellular organisms, including algae, plants, fungi, and animals evolved through compressive accumulation because they had to live attached to the ground.

With respect to multicellular organisms, due to the characteristic of a multicellular body, multicellular organisms inherited endospores and immunity among the elements of survival-related life history, and vertically inherited self-replication, which is a mode of asexual reproduction.

Horizontal gene transfer was inherited only in such a way that it is used in sexual reproduction. Endospores seem to be inherited in the form of a hard survival structure as shown in the sporophytes of algae, the zygotes and sporophytes of fungi, the spores and seeds of plants, and fertilized eggs of animals.

It seems that protists with haploid trophic forms took a path toward evolution into plants through the stage of algae, whereas protists with diploid trophic forms took a path toward evolution into animals. Fungi seem to have taken a similar path, depending on the conditions of each species, such as the number of chromosomes.

Algae and plants undergo alternation of generations and alternate between the haploid gametophyte and diploid sporophyte, as haploid trophic protists alternate between the haploid trophic form and diploid zygote. Thus, the haploid gametophyte can be seen as the multicellularized version of the trophic form of haploid protists, while the sporophyte can be viewed as the multicellularized organism corresponding to the diploid zygote of haploid protists.

The meiosis of sporophytes may also be viewed as a multicellularized version of the meiosis that the diploid zygotes of haploid protists undergo to go back to the original trophic form when the environment becomes favorable again.

Many people are curious about the origin of angiosperms. Regarding the evolution of angiosperms, I think that diploid sporophytes absorbed haploid gametophytes and thereby evolved into diploid gametophytes like animals. Diploid gametophytes evolved into a very competent homologous chromosome system, and they also came to have internal reproductive organs in the body.

Thus, they became able to directly form germ cells, i.e., sperm and eggs, cause germ cells to undergo fertilization, and supply nutrients to fertilized eggs so that they will grow directly into diploid gametophytes, so they do not undergo alternation of generations. This is the reason why the fertilized eggs of animals receive yolks from eggs, and angiosperms form the endosperm through double fertilization and supply nutrients to fertilized eggs that become seeds.

Angiosperms account for 90% of the plants inhabiting the planet, and this is also thought to be due to the fact that they have high developmental plasticity due to the competence of homologous chromosomes that angiosperms possess as diploid gametophytes.

As animals ceased their earlier attachment life and acquired motility, they became able to live and spread all over the planet. This also seems to be due to the competence of the homologous chromosome system. Along with the evolution of angiosperms, the flourishing of insects and flowers has become possible because they both have a short lifespan and share a homologous chromosome system which allows high developmental plasticity.

When diploid gametophytes like animals and angiosperms form germ cells, crossing over of homologous chromosomes inherited from parents occurs. This is thought to occur for the purpose of deriving genetic diversity. Regarding the reason for the existence of homologous chromosomes in multicellular organisms, it can be regarded as the multicellularized version of the process in which haploid trophic protists form diploid zygotes in the process of sexual reproduction.

Diploid trophic protists form germ cells by meiosis during sexual reproduction, immediately undergo the conjugation of germ cells, and return to the diploid trophic form to endure a harsh environment. However, they reproduce by self-replication when the environment becomes favorable.

Diploid multicellular gametophytes still have the essential nature of diploid trophic protists. For this reason, their mode of reproduction is similar to that of diploid trophic protists. In other words, gametophytes form germ cells by meiosis, then the combination of germ cells occurs, and the fertilized egg or the diploid zygote undergoes the numerous processes of somatic cell division to grow into a diploid gamete multicellular organism.

However, when germ cells are formed, DNA editing occurs through crossing over of homologous chromosomes inherited from parents, and meiosis occurs in this state. This seems to be intended to generate genetic diversity by inheriting the horizontal gene transfer of prokaryotes once again but applying it in a modified form suitable for the system of multicellular organisms

In other words, the horizontal gene transfer of prokaryotes occurred for the direct purpose of acquiring the fragments of other genes, but protists inherited this life history for the purpose of acquiring stability as diploid zygotes through the combination of two identical chromosomes.

Among multicellular organisms, dipolid gametophytes inherited the life history once more for the direct purpose of generating genetic diversity among individuals in a species. Therefore, the genetic diversity of multicellular organisms allows individuals to adapt in a unique way. In this respect, genetic diversity itself is the completion of adaptation, and it is unreasonable that it exists to become the target of Darwinian selection again.

Genetic diversity, which allows for diversification of the

methods of adapting to the environment, is very valuable in itself. The biological value of genetic diversity is shown by the fact that fungi perish rather than undergoing conjugation with the same gender with identical genes.

The gametophytes of algae and plants are haploid, and produce germ cells through mitosis, so they cannot have chromosomal crossover like diploid gametophytes. In addition, even when the sporophytes of algae and plants undergo meiosis to form spores, meiosis occurs to allow spores to immediately grow into haploid gametophytes, as when the zygotes of haploid protists undergo meiosis to return to the trophic form.

In this case, meiosis does not occur for the conjugation of spores like germ cells, so there is no need for chromosomal crossover.

## C. The Mechanism of the Speciation: The Use and Disuse of Organs According to the Principle of the Precedence of Survival over Reproduction

**"I really want to see it. Many surprising facts will be revealed. It's a phenomenal thing. Our understanding of nature will become completely different. I believe that there will come a time when the web of life will be**

revealed in a completely different form than we have ever known." (Barbara McClintock. A Feeling for the Organism, a biography of Barbara McClintock by Evelyn Fox Keller)

"However, this (natural selection) alone cannot explain evolution. This is due to the fact that in evolutionary biology, there is a second view that estimates and describes the history of evolution, that is, 'After life came into being in this world, how did it go through continuous changes and evolve into various living things?' This viewpoint argues that only a single principle called natural selection cannot explain the pattern." (Hasegawa Eisuke, *A Fascinating Evolution Story That Will Make You Stay Up All Night*)

I'd like to begin my discussion on speciation by redefining the concept of species. All organisms seek to survive in the first place, and reproduction started as a method for extending survival, so reproduction seems to intrinsically imply that it is concomitant to survival. However, reproduction is also an essential life activity and the evolution of numerous species of organisms existing today would not have been possible without reproduction. Therefore, 'a species' should be defined as 'a group of individuals that share 'survival culture' and 'reproduction culture.'

All species of prokaryotes acquire gene fragments through horizontal gene transfer. Thus, in biology centered on genes, it may be thought that the concept of species is shaken in the case of prokaryotes due to the genetic impurity of prokaryotes. However, I think that there is no need to adhere to such a view. This is the survival life history that shows that organisms evolved to survive well in their environments. Therefore, I think that the definition of species given above can be appropriately applied to all species of three kingdoms.

Meanwhile, considering that the evolutionary theory emerged as a theory on the principle of the speciation of multicellular organisms at an early stage of the development of biology, I'd like to focus my discussion on the speciation of multicellular organisms.

The species of multicellular organisms are frequently divided into two sexes, male and female, but their modes of reproduction involve numerous aspects, such as parthenogenesis including asexual reproduction and sexual reproduction. Even sexual reproduction involves very diverse aspects, such as hermaphrodite organisms, various systems such as monogamy and polygamy, reproduction by the queen, simultaneous existence of haploid gametophytes and diploid gametophytes, seasonal alternation of sexual and asexual reproduction methods, sexes of individuals and sex conversion, inbreeding, and distinct sexual dimorphism. Therefore, it appears that it is very difficult to derive a theory that comprehensively explains all these aspects.

On the other hand, when I found the mechanism of the evolution sex, I realized that it is not possible to discuss the speciation of multicellular organisms without understanding the evolution of sex. This is due to the fact that since speciation is the principle of the formation of male and female members of a species, it inevitably presupposes the concept of sexual reproduction as its premise. I think that to explicate the principle of speciation of multicellular organisms, it is necessary to understand the evolutionary origin of multicellular organisms.

Multicellular organisms include the elements of prokaryotes, which are their ancestor organisms, and at the same time, they are, in essence, multicellularized protists. I think that if we start from this perspective, the principle of speciation can be easily explained.

Based on the above discussion, I will now attempt to discuss the principle of speciation of multicellular organisms. First, regarding the existence of more than two sexes found in some species of protists and fungi, I think it is related to the fact that they can function as reproductive cells themselves without forming germ cells and reproduce sexually by selecting the sex that can derive genetic diversity.

On the other hand, algae, plants and animals have only two sexes, male and female, and these two sexes evolved simultaneously. I think this phenomenon can be understood if we consider the fact that these organisms are still protists in essence except for multicellularity.

As described earlier, protists form only two gametes simultaneously, and it is presumed to be a measure against the overcombination of germ cells. In multicellular organisms, the gametophyte is the multicellular body that forms sperm and eggs, and sperm and eggs are simultaneously produced. In this situation, female and male gametophytes producing them had no choice but to evolve simultaneously, whether they were haploid or diploid. As a result, hermaphrodite animals or plants can exist, and even in dioecious animals or plants, female and male gametes evolved simultaneously.

Protists do not have any sexes because they form two germ cells through mitosis or meiosis. Therefore, in multicellular organisms that evolved from protists through multicellularization, earlier organisms were more frequently hermaphrodite. Even in such cases, they reproduced through cross fertilization for genetic diversity, and subsequently evolved into dioecious animals or plants, which is thought to be a method for ensuring cross fertilization.

Meanwhile, germ cells of all organisms including prokaryotes and protists originate from somatic cells. Even when protists reproduce sexually, trophic forms undergo mitosis or meiosis to form germ cells, whether they are haploid or diploid.

Multicellular organisms cannot be an exception to this principle. When multicellular organisms reproduce asexually, somatic cells reproduce other somatic cells, and sexual reproduction also occurs in a similar way. Therefore, it seems to be a logical view that survival-related and reproductive traits occur in somatic cells and are transmitted from somatic cells to germ cells in multicellular organisms as well as other organisms.

It is a natural phenomenon, considering that only somatic cells, which survive and reproduce in the front line of life, can obtain accurate information required for acquisition of traits, and such information is very difficult for organs other than somatic cells to obtain. When a species of multicellular organisms has found a new ecological niche to adapt to sudden environmental changes or to avoid competition, the species needs to adapt to the new environment and somatic cells confront the changes in the front line. Thus, genetic changes in somatic cells need to occur.

Through my research, I arrived at the conclusion that the evolutionary origin of stem cells is the acquisition of new traits. Stem cells are part of somatic cells of multicellular organisms, and are said to have the property of pursuing cellular homeostatis. The Japanese biologist Susumu Tonegawa found the principle of antibody formation in the immune system of the human body, and this antibody formation occurs in somatic cells. I reasoned that after stem cells have completed both adaptation for survival and reproductive adaptation in a new environment, they will acquire genetic changes for the new environment in a manner similar to the principle of antibody formation.

According to a book on stem cells, after the death of a man who underwent heart transplant surgery and received the heart from a female donor, it was found that a large proportion of his heart cells showed changes in sex chromosomes from XX chromosomes to XY chromosomes, which was thought to be due to the fact that the man's stem cells entered his heart cells and underwent mitosis.

Thus, I inferred that speciation seems to occur as

follows. After stem cells have acquired survival-related and reproductive genetic information suitable for a new ecological niche transmitted from stem cells, the stem cells go into all the cells of the human body, including spermatogonias and ooblasts. Then, spermatogonias and ooblasts seem to transmit genetic information transmitted from stem cells to germ cells, and germ cells formed from spermatogonias and ooblasts undergo fertilization and become fertilized eggs, thereby completing the process of speciation.

Meanwhile, how can stem cells form survival-related information and reproductive information? I think this is the part where 'the law of the use and disuse of organs according to the principle of the precedence of survival over reproduction' comes into play.

In a new ecological niche, all organisms first acquire adaptive traits for survival, such as living individually or in a group depending on the relationships with their food or prey and natural enemies. Then, they reproduce by adopting the mode of reproduction that can transmit the acquired adaptive traits for survival, whether it is asexual reproduction or sexual reproduction, and they thereby acquire adaptive traits for reproduction.

The use and disuse of organs according to the principle of

the precedence of survival over reproduction are the origin of both asexual reproduction described in the previous section and the numerous modes of sexual reproduction following the simultaneous evolution of two sexes, female and male.

They are also the cause of sexual dimorphism of females and males. The principle of the precedence of survival over reproduction is inevitably the order in which the use and disuse of organs occur, and the occurrence of traits of each organ is the consequence.

In species that reproduce by sexual reproduction, it is also the most efficient mode of reproduction concomitant to the mode of survival that organisms have adopted after they have secured their survival culture in their respective ecological niche as an essential element for their existence, females and males acquire and share traits for survival simultaneously.

Thereafter, they also separately acquire reproductive traits at the same time, and these reproductive traits are acquired concomitantly along with survival traits. Although I described the acquisition of reproductive traits as 'concomitant' to the acquisition of traits for survival, the acquisition of reproductive traits occurs almost simultaneously along with the acquisition of traits for survival because speciation generally occurs in a favorable environment that allows survival.

The evidence for the possibility of such a process is the modularity of toolkit genes and genetic switches regulating them in animals, and if they are not viewed as factors that enable simultaneous and large-scale trait changes in the overall body organs, it is difficult to understand their roles.

For example, the reproduction cultures of all the species described below are the results of the use and disuse of organs according to the principle of the precedence of survival over reproduction. Actually, the principle seems to be applied to all the species of three kingdoms, including plants and animals.

Honeybees or ants have an ecological status of living together in a colony. The reason for the way of living of these species is that if the queen is not entirely responsible for reproduction, individual members cannot even have a chance for survival, let alone reproduction. Worker female bees are diploid organisms because they perform a wide range of activities for survival. In comparison, male bees are haploid organisms produced by parthenogenesis because their main role is limited to reproduction.

The simultaneous existence of the diploid female gametophyte and haploid male gametophyte in honey bees is comparable to the alternation between the haploid gametophyte and the diploid sporophyte in plants.

For another example, naked mole rates also live in a safe underground space and maintain their ecological niche. If all female members of the species reproduce, they cannot survive safely in the underground space, so only the queen is solely responsible for reproduction.

For yet another example, clownfish live in small groups in a poisonous sea anemone under the protection of the sea anemone. In a group of clownfish, the individual with the largest body is the only female, and for reproduction, this female mates with the male, which is the second largest individual in the group.

Regarding the reason for this method for reproduction, if all the individuals reproduced in a narrow space, it would be impossible for the clownfish to live safely in the anemone and maintain their ecological niche. In the case of clownfish, females are larger than males, probably because they need to produce eggs with yolks. If the sole female dies, the sex of the largest male changes into female and it mates with the second largest male which becomes mature among the other individuals that are all immature males. This method of reproduction seems to be due to the fact that it is the least expensive method for the survival for the species.

Among mammals, hyenas have an ecological niche as scavengers that will eat anything. In hyenas, females are overwhelmingly stronger than males. This seems to be a result of the evolutional process of hyenas in which female hyenas have fiercely protected themselves and their cubs against predation by males and thus have kept males from preying on females or their offspring since the earlier stages of formation of its species.

Meanwhile, seahorses are known to live by wrapping their tails around seaweed or corals. In this species, not females but males get pregnant. The reason for male pregnancy in seahorses seems to be related to the fact that if seahorses fertilize in the water like other fish species, their sperm and eggs may be drifted away due to the current or may be regarded as prey and eaten by other fish, so it is necessary for them to reproduce by internal fertilization. Their male pregnancy also seems to be due to the fact that if female seahorses not only produce eggs with yolks but also get pregnant, it would not be favorable for their survival.

On the other hand, catfish have settled on streams with

a strong current as their ecological niche, and they are reported to reproduce in such a way that males release sperm into the mouth of females. This mode of reproduction of catfish also provides a typical example of the use and disuse of organs according to the principle of the precedence of survival over reproduction.

With respect to bird species, in peacocks and birds of paradise, males have an overwhelmingly beautiful appearance. This seems to be due to the fact that males need to focus all energy on attracting and courting females because females alone lay eggs and raise offspring, which is possible because their environment for survival in terms of their ecological niche is very favorable for their survival and they are very intelligent. In other words, sexual dimorphism in these bird species is the result of focusing all energy on reproductive adaptation in an environment that there is little need for survival adaptation.

Darwin's evolutionary theory claims that mutations happen to occur in germ cells without any experience of living an actual life, they are selected by nature, and as a result, evolution occurs. Darwinism suggests that a very rare thing like a windfall has been transformed into an ordinary event in everyday life. This theory cannot provide a valid explanation of speciation.

In addition, it cannot explain the reason why numerous species are formed through adaptive radiation. If mutations are endlessly selected by nature as Darwinian theories explains, there would be no need for the formation of species, and even if a species is formed, it would be disintegrated and disappear soon.

In Darwin's evolutionary theory, individuals play a central role in reproduction, so Darwinism cannot explain the evolution of reproduction by the queen in species such as honeybees and ants. Darwin is said to have predicted that his theory would be disproved if a future theory provides an appropriate explanation of the evolution of species in which the queen is entirely responsible for reproduction.

According to Darwin's evolutionary theory and genetic determinism proposed by Richard Dawkins, which presented a similar viewpoint to Darwinism, organisms are passive machines led by genes. However, real living organisms were active beings in that they evolved sexual reproduction by inheriting the life history of ancestor organisms, formed an ecological niche to ensure stable survival, and reproduce by the method that did not hinder survival after securing survival.

After all, Lamarckism was not erroneous in any way. Lamarck's evolutionary theory argued that evolution occurred through the simultaneous evolution of females and males of a species and the acquisition and inheritance of traits of somatic cells through the use and disuse of organs. Based on his evolutionary theory, I only added the principle of the precedence of survival over reproduction.

In short, there was no room for selection in evolution, whether it is natural selection or sexual selection, and evolution only shows the traces of the earnest life of living organisms trying to adapt to the environment. In Lamarckism and my evolutionary theory, organisms with neurons and the brain that induce behaviors leading to evolution can restore their position as active agents in the actual life and evolution.

Although all species inherit habits and organs formed by their ancestors through genes, at the same time, they are able to adapt successfully to environmental changes if necessary at any time. They may thereby become ancestors of new species, and subsequently pass down their acquired traits to their descendants.

However, I want to emphasize that since evolution is a species-level biological event, the cooperation of members of the relevant species is important.

## D. Brain-Based Personality Type Hypothesis

The neurons or the brain of animals developed due to the need to sense the environment, form sensory information and connect the information with movement.

The emergence of mammals led to the development of positive and negative emotions, which resulted in the evolution of the amygdala. Also, when emotions were combined with sensory information about the environment, memory came into being, which led to the evolution of the hippocampus. In addition, primates evolved the thinking ability of processing and using memories, which resulted in the evolution of the frontal lobe.

The explosive growth of the human brain including the frontal lobe occurred over a relatively short period of about 2.5 million years in the history of human evolution. It is believed to be a result of humans' domination of the environment primarily through the use of the thinking ablity. I also think that this phenomenon can be explained by nothing other than the effects of the use and disuse of organs.

In thinking, existing information such as memory is consciously employed. Therefore, I reasoned that when the frontal lobe is used, the operation of the amygdala stops. As a result, the frontal lobe and the amygdala are thought to be selectively operated, although it is not easy to distinguish between the operations of the two organs. In the course of evolution, humans have been aware of the natural environment well by using their thinking ability, and as a result, when the frontal lobe was used, the operation of the amygdala almost stopped.

However, the amygdala of the human brain operates actively in modern society, and this may be attributed to the fact that as the environment of mankind has become excessively complex, human beings' ability to control the environment has been decreased and thus their anxiety has been increased.

In addition, I hypothesized that after we human beings evolved language, humans evolved into persons of two personality types, rational and emotional types, as a result of the use and disuse of organs through the power of language as the means of human thinking.

In addition, I think that rational people predominantly use the frontal lobe of the brain, whereas emotional people predominantly use the amygdala of the brain. Further, according to my theory, since rational persons predominantly use the frontal lobe, they have a better thinking ability but have a lower empathic ability.

For emotional people, they have a lower power of the frontal lobe and a better empathic ability, but since they have a weaker thinking ability, they are more likely to suffer from depression. Regarding people with emotional personality traits, I thought that if they change their pattern of using the brain in such a way that they predominantly use the frontal lobe, it will reduce the operation of the amygdala, so they will probably be able to cure their depression.

By applying this method to myself, I was able to overcome my depression in a relatively short time. In this connection, it should be noted that I was able to easily apply the behavior patterns of these personality types to my own behaviors because I am familiar with rational personality types. I gained a better understanding of such personality types as a result of having dealt with divorces cases as a lawyer for a long time.

I think that since a married couple is the unit of adaptation in human beings, people with opposite personality types get married in an attempt to complement themselves. I also think that since personality is such a strong biological trait that it is generally difficult to overcome, so personality differences between a husband and his wife occur, leading to marital conflicts.

In short, if we find biological principles behind married couples' union, that is, if we can understand the reason for the marriage of people with opposite personality types and the principle of the operation of rational and emotional personalities, we will get clues to resolving marital conflicts. After all, I was able to overcome my marital problems by applying this theory to my marriage life.

### E. Related Issues

Biology is a truly important field of science since it explains the life of all organisms on the planet as it is. However, biological theories based on Darwin's evolutionary theory are in conflict with the creationism of Christians, and evolutionary psychology derived from social biology is in discord with feminism. In addition, they do not provide a biological justification or explanation for sexual minorities such as homosexuals and abortions.

However, my new evolutionary theory, 'the use and disuse of organs according to the principle of the precedence of survival over reproduction', gives an appropriate explanation for all these phenomena.

Homosexuality is a typical phenomenon that follows the principle of the precedence of survival over reproduction, and this phenomenon evolved because human beings, who adapt to the environment by using intelligence, place more importance on interpersonal relationships than on childbirth and child rearing.

In the new evolutionary theory, speciation occurs through genetic changes that result from the behaviors of animals with neurons or the brain, so this theory suggests that the identity of individuals lies in their brain.

As a result, regarding the fact that among human beings, transgender people perceive their gender as the opposite one of their biological sex, we can provide the explanation that the true sexual identity of transgender people lies in the brain. In other words, the true gender of transgender people is the gender that they perceive to be their own.

The adaptation of organisms occurs through the use and disuse of organs in accordance with the principle of the precedence of survival over reproduction. Therefore, according to the principle, like other species, human beings first acquired traits for survival, such as intelligence, and subsequently acquired reproductive traits manifested by the sexual dimorphism of today's males and females.

Since there are no gender differences in survival traits, feminism seems to be based on biology, but it should be noted that reproductive traits are also very strong biological traits because they have become adaptive traits of our species.

The controversy or debate around feminism, which has recently become a serious social issue, is thought to result from a lack of understanding of the distinction between survival traits and reproductive traits.

In other words, this problem is a phenomenon arising from a situation where women focus on survival traits and men focus on reproductive traits. However, I have no idea of the specific arguments or specific viewpoints of those involved in the debate or conflicts around feminism.

In relation to current controversy about feminism, I think both biologists and feminists should make efforts to resolve related problems one by one by increasing public awareness and deriving public consensus through public discussion.

However, women's abortions are thought to be a typical phenomenon that reflects the principle of the precedence of survival over reproduction. In this connection, South Africa's Cape fur seals are reported to abort in large numbers when their food is scarce, and this phenomenon indicates that women's abortions are a phenomenon that occurs when childbirth threatens women's adaptation for survival.

Theistic religions are believed to be a supreme scientific phenomenon because they are humanity's adaptive traits for survival that human beings have formed through the use and disuse of organs in an attempt to overcome ignorance or suffering in the course of adapting to the environment.

In a sense, the adaptation of organisms to the environment is merely part of the behavior of living things that live on the ground, eat food, produce excreta, and reproduce. However, only human beings seek the meaning of life while trying to communicate with omnipotent God, who dwells in a high place. It is an undeniable fact that this aspect of humans is a very special and surprising adaptation trait of our species.

Creationism or theology is a study that systematizes the contents about giving mystical power to God and expressing appreciation to and worshipping God at the same time. Thus, it deserves to be called the pinnacle of humanities and must be viewed as an adaptation phenomenon in which the uniqueness of ethology of our species Homo sapiens has been exerted.

Homo sapiens is the species that has evolved into the most intelligent beings on the planet, and countless numbers of people belonging to Homo sapiens believe in God. Given this fact, I think that it is absurd to claim that theistic religions are based on a mere unscientific delusion.

## Origin of Sex, and the Fates of
## Lamarckism and Darwinism

PowerKorea met Kwon Sung-hee, who published a book titled <The Evolution Of Sex Through The Inheritance Of Life History And Speciation As A Result Of The Use And Disuse Of Organs>

One of the biggest problems biologists have faced to solve is why animals are divided into male and female and plants into pistil and stamen? They call this phenomenon 'sexual reproduction'. Many biologists, west or east, have challenged to bring up answers but they all have failed. Interestingly, a South Korean family lawyer attorney has brought up an answer to this. The name of this amateur biologist is Sunghee Kwon.

She says that she has found the mechanism of sexual reproduction and the speciation cannot be discussed without knowing the evolution of sex, and asserts Darwin is wrong and Lamarck is right. Thus she gained a nickname 'the daughter of Lamarck'. She explained her findings and reasons of her assertions in her book <The Evolution Of Sex

Through The Inheritance Of Life History And Speciation As A Result Of The Use And Disuse Of Organs> (August 2021). While she is preparing her findings to be evaluated by those who have profound knowledge in the field, monthly <PowerKorea> sat down with her and learned about her findings.

**Q1. First of all, you are a family law attorney. It's interesting that you published a book about biological evolution rather than law. What's the story behind this?**

I've dealt with a lot of divorce cases and many of them complained about personality clash. One day, I was struck with a question: why did they get married anyway because they knew they were different at first hand? During the course of my curiosity, I myself faced a divorce. Then I thought that there might be some biological reasons behind this.

So, I sampled 100 couples of my clients. To my surprise, 65 couples had stark differences in personality. I then started digging books about biology and evolution. And I came to a conclusion that humans evolved into two types in personality: rational and emotional. The rational uses frontal lobe and the emotional amygdala each dominantly.

And I thought the reason a male (or female) marries to an opposite personality comes from a natural desire to make up for one's weak point. I approached this with biological principles and applied them to me and my husband's case first. We still remain together happily, and highly likely, ever after.

**Q2. Very interesting. So, your book contains your experience as an attorney and biological findings?**

Before publishing the book, I read about 400 books about biology and evolution for 5 years. During the course of my study, I encountered Darwin's natural selection and sexual selection but with great doubts: those whom nature favors survive and thrive, and those whom nature disfavors likely to disappear; the splendid feathers of a male peacock were evolved as such because a female peacock chose him? I think this idea of him is against the essence of life.

Lamarck's theory of use and disuse of organs by inner will at least is better than this as it backs up 'independence' of individual organisms that serves survival and reproduction which is more closely related to the essence of life. My doubts in Darwin's grew as much as my support to Lamarck's. So, the book contains these stories and my own findings.

**Q3. We learned that you found 'the mechanism of evolution of sex' and 'the mechanism of speciation'. Please enlighten us.**

This might be a difficult part for ordinary people to understand but I'll try my best. In the order of evolution, organisms are divided into prokaryotes, protists and multicellular organisms. Protists emerged from prokaryotes eating each other and lived communally in division of nucleus and mitochondria. Multicellular organisms emerged from protists acquiring multicellular factors in the course of evolution.

What I found is a phenomenon that protists and multicellular organisms inherit life history of prokaryotes according to the structures of their body and dielectric. A good example of this is asexual reproduction (a reproduction that does not need the union of sex cells or gametes unlike in sexual reproduction where male and female gametophytes are needed). Protists often form cysts when the environment is harsh and the same can be found in cysts of moss and fern, seeds of angiosperm, and fertilized eggs of insects getting through the winter. I understood this as inheriting life history of bacteria's endospore.

I also found that sexual reproduction has walked the same path as this that evolved by creatively using life history of ancestors in order to better survive and reproduce. Prokaryotes replicate, forms endospore, and does horizontal gene transfer. Protists forms reproductive cells to join and fuse cells into the solid survival structure in harsh winter and proliferate when warm spring comes. In other words, protists use these three life histories of prokaryotes to evolve sexual reproduction. This is a revolutionary method that organisms on Earth survive and thrive in hard times.

Among multicellular organisms, animals and angiosperms are diploid gametophytes which have reproductive organs that produce sperms and eggs. When they produce sperms and eggs, they cross their parents' chromosomes which are the same in application of the prokaryotes' horizontal gene migration according to the systems of multicellular organisms once more. Genetic diversity comes from this application.

The key to understand evolution of sex is that the descendants still have the factor of prokaryotes, thus the factor works when necessary. In order to understand the mechanism of speciation, we need to understand the mechanism of evolution of sex first. Speciation is but the principle to decide male and female in species.

Protists make two germ cells simultaneously to prevent

deformity or infertility. Multicellular organisms also make sperms and eggs simultaneously. In multicellular organisms, gametophytes like male and female are to produce sperms and eggs. Therefore male and female evolve simultaneously.

This simultaneous formation is the principle of speciation which we can observe in hermaphrodites or gonochorism. The findings of 'the mechanism of evolution of sex' and 'the mechanism of speciation' occurred to me intuitively after years of extensive reading and close observations.

**Q4. Ok. We also learned about your 'the survival first and reproduction later principle' as a new theory of evolution. Can you tell us about it?**

Survival is the top priority of all living things on Earth. All of their actions including reproduction do not intend to go against survival. Gathering all of my knowledge and observations, I can say that all living organisms including prokaryotes, protists and multicellular organisms follow this principle. I call this 'the survival first and reproduction later principle'.

This survival first and reproduction later principle applies regardless methods of reproduction whether it is parthenogenesis, incest, monogamy, polygamy or polyandry.

An example is that bees, naked mole-rats, and clark's anemonefish reproduce by representative females in order to survive and to maintain the order of the system. Without the reproduction of the queens, the members of the species even cannot have chances to survive far from reproducing.

And this survival first and reproduction later principle is combined inseparably with Lamarck's law of use and disuse of organs in order. For example, species decide the ecological niches to avoid competition, the survival organs are made first among male and female simultaneously as a result of survival first behaviors and reproductive organs are made separately for both male and female subsequently as a result of reproduction later behaviors.

Thus the sexual dimorphism is exactly the result of the survival first and reproduction later principle. We can observe this principle in many living things in many living environments: female hyenas are stronger than male, male sea dragons getting pregnant instead of female, etc. The reason feathers of male peacocks and birds of paradise are extremely beautiful is because their habitats are well provided and females can rear offspring, males focus on seducing females.

The secrecy of speciation is that multicellular organisms

remain as protists when multicellularity is removed. The germ cells of protists are produced from the somatic cells. The sperms and eggs of multicellular also come from somatic cells which they get the traits by the use and disuse of organs based on the survival first and reproduction later principle. For example, the human antibody is formed in somatic cells.

The Darwin and Dawkins' genetic determination treat all living organisms as 'passive' machines dragged by genes. But in fact, living things on Earth inherited life history of their ancestors, evolved through securing ecological niche and lived on the survival first and reproduction later principle on which I assert that they are 'active' beings. If my theory of evolution and Lamarck's law of use and disuse gain academic recognition, all living things that have neurons and brains will recover their disvalued independence.

**Q5. At this point, we are curious about how your findings can be related to our real life.**

The human race is just a species that lives on Earth, eat and release, the quintessential desire of all animals. Yet, they are the only species who try to find meanings of life through reaching out to God. This phenomenon, I think, is the 'ultimate of science'. God is our marvelous scientific companion who raises existence of our beings to a different dimension, and thus the creationism is the highest praise devoted to God from us, the humans. How can we, therefore, assert that this creationism is a mere delusion built based on unscientific facts?

Darwin's theory of evolution is causing conflicts among biologists, evolutionary psychology, divine creation of the world, and feminism. It doesn't give biological answers to homosexuality and abortion either.

But 'the survival first and reproduction later principle' and the Lamarck's law of use and disuse of organs can explain all of these phenomena. For example, survival traits like intelligence get equally first for both male of female and therefore feminism (gender equality in economic and social activities) lays its principle at this biological survival first. In other words, human society has responsibility to systematically take care of pregnant female workers from any possible discrimination and disadvantages.

For another example, homosexuality is a phenomenon that intelligent humans value relationship more than reproduction and rearing offspring, while abortion can also be explained as an act of surviving first because giving a birth can be survival threatening to women.

**Q6. You are an ardent supporter of Lamarck's and a resistance to Darwin's. What do you think are the respond of the academic world at the moment?**

Well, I'm an amateur biologist with only 5 years of study in the field. I published the book only 2 months ago and I'm expecting to see how the academic world will respond to my findings and assertions. So, I'm actually looking forward to hearing it.

**Q7. Are you frequently engaging with scholars in the field?**

I read hundreds of biology books. Sadly, most biologists seem to take sides with Darwin. So, I lost motivation to engage with them as I have great doubts about his theory. However, I wrote a paper <Hypothesis on Personality Types of Frontal Lobe Dominant and Amygdala Dominant>. I was invited to present the paper at the HBES conference. Then my father passed away and I couldn't make it. But I can say that the paper is one of a kind try in the field.

It is also hopeful that as inheritance of acquired characteristics is being recognized again among academic circles through epigenetics, Lamarck is also coming into the center of attention.

## Q8. Lastly, what is your next move as a biologist?

I'm greatly interested in Homo sapiens as evolutionary beings. I didn't untangle much of my thoughts about humans, their biometrics and characteristics in the book. So, I want to make them all in my next book.

I'm also thinking of writing a book about God and creation viewed from scientific perspective. One thing I would like to ask <PowerKorea> readers is that my findings of 'the mechanism of evolution of sex' and 'the mechanism of speciation' must be good news to the scientific world and I encourage you to spread the news to as many biologists as possible around you.

## The 21st century is the time for President Macron's France

*I have a will to lead France to benefit the world, a cosmic aspiration.*
- From Revolution by Emmanuel Macron

I am writing this letter to President Emmanuel Macron and Ambassador Philippe Lefort of the French Embassy in Korea regarding the biologist Jean-Baptiste Lamarck. First, I would like to express my deep respect to President Macron and Ambassador Philippe Lefort. It is known that President Macron has been accomplishing 'Macron Revolution' in the French Republic, the native country of Jeanne d'Arc loved by God and the country of great people who earned freedom, equality and fraternity through the French Revolution. I am a Korean lawyer (vice president of the Korean Bar Association), an amateur biologist who wrote a book on evolutionary biology, and an advocate of God sent by Jesus. I have nicknames such as Kwon d'Arc and the daughter of Lamarck, and these nicknames are related to my research on evolutionary biology.

Considering that I am a Korean amateur biologist, you may wonder why I am writing this letter to French politicians. I am writing this letter because the Lord gave me a revelation and ordered me to inform you that the 21st century is the time of President Macron's France.

First, this letter is related to the restoration of the honor and reputation of Jean Batiste Lamarck (1744~1829), a French biologist. Lamarck greatly contributed to the development of biology and proposed the theory of evolution. As you probably know, there is a statue of Lamarck in 'le Jardin des Plantes de Paris' ('the Garden of Plants of Paris') designed by Lamarck. The statue contains the sculpted image of Lamarck and his daughter and an inscription at the base. The inscription reads as follows: 'Posterity will admire you. Posterity will avenge you, father.' You may know about this. If a French person is receiving unfair treatment internationally, isn't it a problem that should be dealt with by French politicians such as the president or diplomats of France? Even though Lamarck is not alive, considering his position in France, I believe that if it is found that his theory and reputation has been unjustly tarnished for 200 years, this problem should be addressed by politicians like you.

Lamarck's innovative idea that organisms evolve did not fit the ethos of the time when Christianity had a strong influence on society. In those days, the creationist views of scientists such as Georges Cuvier, a paleontologist and creationist, prevailed. Thus, Lamarck' theory received little recognition by scientists during his life, and he died miserably. His theory served as a basis of Charles Darwin's evolutionary theory in England. However, after the presence of genes and gene mutations were predicted and confirmed later, difficulty in explicating the detailed mechanism became an obstacle to the restoration of his reputation as a biologist. Subsequently, he was subjected to unjust ridicule and mortification by scientists that could not tolerate the shadow of God in science, and his evolutionary theory is still being unjustly ridiculed even today. According to Darwin's evolutionary theory, mutations occur randomly without any directions in reproductive cells that do not have any experience of living. The theory also claims that such mutations are selected by nature and reproductions are repeated. Regarding mutations that are not selected by nature and thus disappear, I find it difficult to understand that organisms create mutations that will never be used. However, since Darwin's theory is far from divine interventions in the life of organisms, it was better suited to the taste of scientists.

I work as a divorce lawyer in Korea, and when I was conducting my personal research on personality differences of married couples from the perspective of evolutionary biology in 2017, I encountered the theories proposed by Lamarck and Darwin. While studying their theories, I became convinced that their positions in biology should be reversed. Therefore, I started to delve into evolutionary biology in an attempt to find true facts about the evolution of organisms. I began to study biology because I couldn't accept Darwin's evolutionary theory that regards organisms merely as machines led by genes rather than viewing them as active agents that adapt themselves to the environment. I work as a lawyer in Korea, and lawyers are generally considered intellectuals with a high educational level in Korea as in your country. I perused 400 books in the diverse fields of biology for 5 years. During this period, I devoted all my spare time to biological study and even avoided going out as much as possible to find time for reading. As a result, I was able to prove that Lamarck was right after I revealed the mechanism of the evolution of sex, which is one of the unresolved conundrums in biology. I suppose that since evolution is the speciation by which males and females as the members of a species are formed, there was a need to first elucidate the mechanism of sexual reproduction. To summarize the results of my biological research, I wrote a book titled '*The Evolution of Sex through the Inheritance of*

*Life History and Speciation as a Result of the Use and Disuse of Organs'* (published in August, 2021).

Sexual reproduction was evolved by protists (eukaryotic unicellular organisms). These organisms primarily attempted to survive in unfavorable environments and reproduced only under favorable environmental conditions. In such processes of survival and reproduction, they inherited a combination of habits (life history) of prokaryotes, which are ancestors of protists, and applied the life history in a modified form to make it suitable for the system of descendant organisms (Please first refer to the attached December 2021 issue of PowerKorea, and refer to my book for further details). I found that all living things, including prokaryotes, protists and multicellular organisms, live according to the principle of the precedence of survival over reproduction in that all organisms try to primarily survive in their given environment and reproduce only after ensuring stable survival by adopting the more suitable mode of reproduction between asexual and sexual reproduction. Sexual reproduction also evolved as a result of such modes of existence of organisms according to the principle of the precedence of survival over reproduction. From the perspective of genes, the principle can be called the precedence of metabolism over replication.

Multicellular organisms evolved when protists acquired the multicellularization factor through sedimentation. Haploid protists evolved into plants and diploid protists evolved into animals. This evolution was achieved in the process of seeking survival first before reproduction, and when survival was secured, organisms sought to adopt the more favorable mode of reproduction between sexual and asexual reproduction. If the multicellularization factor is removed from multicellular organisms, they are essentially protists, and the sexual reproduction mode of multicellular organisms evolved through the process of inheriting the life history of prokaryotes in a modified form to make it suitable for the system of multicellular organisms. With respect to the secrets of the evolution of angiosperms, monoploid gametophytes were absorbed by diploid sporophytes, ceased the alternation of generations, and became competent diploid gametophytes like animals. Since diploid gametophytes have a competent system of homologous chromosomes, they supply nutrients (yolks in animals and endosperms in angiosperms) to fertilized eggs, and fertilized eggs directly grow into diploid gametophytes, so the alternation of generations does not occur. I think that animals acquired motility at an early stage of evolution for the same reason.

The reason why multicellular organisms have two sexes, male and female, is not different from the reason why protists have two types of germ cells, sperms and eggs. This is due to the fact that the gametophytes of multicelluar organisms are the multicellularized bodies of protists that produce germ cells. Regarding the presence of two sexes in multicellular organisms and two types of germ cells in protists, the reason I discovered is as follows. When there are more than two types of germ cells, detection for conjugation between the matching two germ cells is delayed, so conjugation (fertilization) takes more time. Moreover, due to difficulty in distinguishing types of germ cells, there is a higher risk of the overcombination of germ cells, and this may produce multiploid gametophytes like triploid gametophytes, which causes deformities or infertility. The presence of only two types of germ cells is the method for preventing these problems. In other words, becoming female or male gametophytes (females and males) is not an inevitable result, but it depends on the coincidentally determined production of sperms or eggs in the distribution process of germ cells. In addition, specific behaviors for reproduction by females and males are performed in a way that they do not invade the mode of survival of the species according to the ecological niche, and the appearance of the species is the result of these ways of living. Since animals are capable of movement, in principle, animal species are gonochoric, which means that animal species have two sexes, male and female, and individuals remain male or female throughout their lives. In contrast, plants are hermaphrodites due to the difficulty of fertilization, but they reproduce by cross pollination, which allows plants to acquire genetic diversity favorable for adaptation.

According to Lamarckism, the internal needs of organisms vary depending on environmental changes, so the use and disuse of organs become different from the existing ones, which lead to the acquisition of new traits, and evolution is completed when both males and females of a species acquire the acquired traits simultaneously. Lamarckism was defeated by Darwinism because it was not able to explain the evolution of female and male sexes. However, because I have identified the principle of formation of female and male sexes, Lamarckism has irreversibly defeated Darwinism this time. More specifically, according to the principle of use and disuse in the order of the precedence of survival over reproduction, both male and female members of a species almost simultaneously acquire traits (organs) for survival, and as they also acquire reproductive traits (organs) separately along with traits for survival, the process of speciation is completed. After all, among all the existing evolutionary theories, only Lamarckism has universality. What I found recently is that survival takes precedence over reproduction regarding the order of the use and disuse of organs. Eventually, acquired traits are acquired by somatic cells (stem cells) and transmitted to germ cells. Genes are only the basis and traces of the behaviors of somatic cells, and reproduction is to replicate not genes but fertilized germ cells (prototypical single cells).

Speciation occurs only when an ecological status is secured in a new environment, so it can be said that the acquisition of reproductive traits occurs almost simultaneously along with the acquisition of traits for survival. In short, a species can be redefined as a population of individuals that share the method of survival and the mode of reproduction. Each species of living organisms has its ecological niche. This fact shows that 'the exclusion of competition' is a biological principle in contrast to the world view based on 'competition for survival' as proposed by Darwinism. The formation of each species itself is a measure for excluding competition since competition is absolutely unfavorable for survival.

Competition occurs only when it is essential for survival for the individuals of a species to live together in groups. When organisms live in groups, competition occurs inevitably. However, even in such cases, determining the territory or ranks of individuals is a strategy for excluding competitions to increase the likelihood of survival by preventing frequent competitions.

Now, don't my explanations sufficiently show that Lamarck has returned along with his daughter? However, in this part, I would like to ask President Macron and Ambassador Lefort to help me. Although it is difficult to make a scientific discovery that has great biological significance, it is much more difficult for biological findings to be officially recognized by the scientific community. For example, endosymbiotic theory, which is now generally recognized as the origin of eukaryotes, was first proposed by a Russian biologist in 1905. However, it did not receive recognition as a valid theory until the American female biologist Lynn Margulis officially introduced it to the scientific community of biologists in the 1960s. Endosymbiotic theory argues that the earliest forms of protists evolved through predation between prokaryotes. This suggests that multicellular organisms as well as protists are still prokaryotes in essence. Thus, it is also an adequate basis of my insight that descendant organisms inherited the life history of prokaryotes. The American female geneticist Barbara McClintock, who can be definitely regarded as a Lamarckian biologist, first published her discovery of 'jumping genes' in 1950 but her finding was recognized in 1980. McClintock mentioned in the 1980s that she was convinced that the web of life would appear in a completely different form than the Darwinian gene-centered form. I'm sure that it refers to the world centered on living organisms that I am describing now.

My findings are not likely to be known and recognized without resorting to an unusual method like my writing this letter. Then, it is also difficult to expect that Lamarck's evolutionary theory will be reevaluated by scientists, and there would be no possibility for the realization of his daughter's prediction that posterity will avenge his father. Since I am an amateur biologist from a country that has not produced great scientific accomplishments in biology so far, there is little possibility that my findings would be recognized by scientists in the world in the near future. However, Lamarck deserves to be called the father of biology considering that he derived the universal theory of evolution through intuition only by observational research on the evolution of invertebrates in 1809. I hope that my findings will serve as a starting point for reexamining and reevaluating Lamarck's theory. I sincerely hope that its scientific validity will be scientifically verified through a meticulous comparison between Lamarckism and Darwinism in your country. In addition, I desire that Lamarck will not be subject to unfair persecution and ridicule any longer and be duly respected as a great biologist eternally in the future.

To this end, I intend to make a suggestion as follows. In most cases of scientific discovery, the process of making a discovery is difficult but the contents of findings are often easy to understand. Typical examples of this tendency include the mechanism of sexual reproduction and the mechanism of speciation that I discovered. Thus, I implore you to provide an opportunity for public discussion so that the general public as well as scientists can participate in the deliberation and determination of the scientific validity of my findings. So far, Darwinism has held a kind of divine status and has been immune to criticism among scientists. It is irrational and incomprehensible that even though scientists fiercely attack the dogmatism of creationism, they do not even question the dogmatism of their own knowledge. Don't you think that they can be called obstinate followers of a religion called

Darwinism? I cannot trust scientists obstinately adhering to Darwinism even though they are scientists from your country. I want to publish my scientific findings as soon as possible not because of the fear of Darwinists' obstruction but because of their unscientific and obstinate attitude.

Actually, Darwin predicted that his theory would be disproved when there emerges a person who can elucidate the evolution of ants in the future. Darwin's theory argues that a species is established through the process in which individual mutations are selected and reproduction is repeated. This theory is difficult to apply to ants since only the queen is responsible for reproduction in a colony. Ants choose to live in a limited space, so if the queen were not entirely responsible for breeding and all female ants reproduced themselves, ants would not maintain their ecological niche. Then, the members of the ant colony would not even have a chance of survival. Thus, it can be said that ants live according to the principle of the precedence of survival over reproduction. This principle also applies to the clownfish, a fish species, and the naked mole rat, a mammal species.

Now, I would like to explain the second reason why I am writing this letter. On June 25 of this year, the U.S.

Supreme Court's decision to overturn Roe v. Wade imposed considerable restrictions on American women's abortions, and President Macron immediately expressed compassion for the situation of American women. Who can help these women? President Macron has been selected by God to help them as an honorable mission to serve the Lord. France sent the Statue of Liberty to the U.S. in 1886, but at this time, President Macron will actually present American women with freedom as their fundamental right. The idea of writing this letter suddenly occurred to me on June 29, when I received a phone call from one of my friends, who works at a foreign embassy. Then, on July 5, Jesus Christ gave me a strong warning about the significance of this opportunity. I was surprised by the revelation and tried to learn about the history of France, the book *Revolution* by President Macron, the history of Jeanne d'Arc, and the book *The Life of Jesus* by Ernest Renan. While I was learning about France, the country where people of unique esprit live, I was very impressed and greatly touched by various facts about France and its people. I also realized that President Macron has been chosen by the Lord because President Macron, who represents authentic French people, is fearlessly realizing the spirit of the French Revolution through 'President Macron's revolution.' I think that the spirit of the French Revolution is to contribute to the prosperity and well-being of all humanity around the world. Since the Lord always loves truth, He specially loves France, whose people love truth, and thus sent Jeanne d'Arc to King Charles VII. In the light of this historical fact, don't you think that it is inevitable that the Lord sent me, Kwon d'Arc, who discovered the biological validity of Lamarckism, to the president of France, who is capable of proclaiming new truth to humanity? What do you think of my view?

Jesus Christ first appeared to me when I was 20 years old, and I had heard his voice two more times before last year. However, since the time when I almost finished writing my book last year, I have heard the voice of Jesus more frequently. (Actually, hundreds of questions occurred to my mind when writing the book for a year, and I received the Lord's answers to each question in the form of a sentence in less than 24 hours. When I told people that I found the secret of the evolution of two sexes, people responded that it was the realm of God. Then, I finally realized that God had always been with me when I found 'the principles of the evolution of sex and a new principle of speciation', which can be said to explain the mode of existence of all organisms.) Christ declared that the 21st century is the era of President

Macron's France and ordered President Macron to perform a leading role in solving various current problems in the world. The method for solving the problems is to make a scientific paradigm shift in order to restore the life view based on active roles of organisms through the reevaluation of Lamarckism. Conservative Christians are opposed to abortions, so I prayed to and asked Jesus Christ to show me His true will through a revelation through a dream. In response to my prayer, the Lord gave me a dream in which I was deeply frustrated due to a totally strange child calling me Mom and the subsequent appearance of a complete stranger claiming that he is my husband. Through the dream, the Lord showed clearly to me that he is not on the side of conservative Christians but on the side of American women as President Macron is. I sincerely request President Macron not to neglect this calling from the Lord and hope that he will enjoy honor following his pursuit of God's calling.

According to Darwinism, there is only passive reproduction (replication) in the life of all organisms, so the Darwinian theory of evolution cannot explain the biological meanings of women's abortions and sexual minorities. However, from the perspective of Lamarckism, each organism forms an ecological niche for stable survival by using its internal needs, and both females and males live according to the principle of survival over reproduction. According to Lamarckism, all the actions of living things are the results of environmental adaptation of organisms. For example, although Darwinian scientists dismiss the concept of God as delusional, the concept of God evolved simultaneously as Homo sapiens evolved language in the course of human evolution. The use of language means living by using knowledge (awareness), which is constituted of the total sum of words with concepts, and knowledge inevitably entails ignorance (the absence of knowledge). As Homo sapiens were striving to deal with ignorance, the transcendental being evolved as a result. Analysis and systemization by language led to the evolution of the criteria of thinking, such as fairness and good and evil (right and wrong), and the transcendental being evolved into the being representing the supreme qualities of the above criteria, i.e., the being representing perfection, the highest good, wisdom, and omnipotence, that is, God. Since the species Homo sapiens is humans, the transcendental being or God evolved into a being that is our companion with human characters, and behaves as a being with human characters.

Therefore, God is undeniably present as a scientific

companion essential for the life of our species Homo sapiens. Due to this nature of God, it can be said that He is the consummate scientific being. As we humans heard God's voice during the time of the Old Testament and during the days of Jeanne d'Arc, we can hear it even today, and this miracle occurred between Jesus Christ and me. As God's advocate, whom Jesus promised to send as written in John chapter 16, I have a duty to proclaim the new truth, such as the principles of human adaptation and the principles of evolution of living things. Although the evolution of living organisms is basically not a process of seeking perfection, there is a tendency that organisms make more efforts than existing species when forming a new ecological niche to adapt to the environmental changes or to avoid competition. As a result, organisms evolved gradually into more intelligent species over time. Finally, Homo sapiens, the most intelligent being on the Earth, emerged and one of them, Jesus Christ polished divine attributes and became God. The human evolution was thereby completed. The view that Jesus came to us as a human was presented by Ernst Renan, a French intellectual, in his book '*The Life of Jesus*' one hundred seventy years ago. This is also my position as a scientist.

On the other hand, although the evolution of language

by humans is a very special human accomplishment in the course of human evolution, language can be basically regarded as simply translating information perceived and processed by biological systems, such as audio and visual signals, into language and applying it. Unlike other animals, we humans need to apply biologically perceived information by translating it each time we use the information, so the speed of human activities has been naturally decreased to a considerable extent. This is why we can't even catch a mosquito with our bare hands. Thus, I think that 'consciousness refers to bio-information translated into language.' On the other hand, language has inherent functions such as analysis and systematic organization, and thus it allows humans to distinguish between good and evil and between beautiful and hideous. However, humans' use of language does not mean that humans can become perfect like God. If humans could become perfect like God only because of their ability to use language, the evolution of God would not have occurred along with the evolution of humans. From an evolutionary perspective, God and man are twins or the two sides of the same coin. In other words, perfect God exists to help imperfect humans. The justices of the U.S. Supreme Court overlooked this point. To rectify this problem, I have now been sent as an advocate of Jesus by Him, and President Macron, who is leading France inhabited by people with their own esprit, has been chosen as a co-worker with God.

Ironically, although creationists and Darwinian evolutionists are currently antagonistic towards each other, they are actually working together in a strong and close-knit alliance. It is due to the fact that this is occurring in a Darwinian paradigm. Creationists disapprove of and castigate women's abortions, and they persecute sexual minorities including homosexuals and transgender people, based on their belief that humans created by God are only males with an XY pair of chromosomes and females with an XX pair of chromosomes. From the perspective of Lamarckism, sexual minorities are also completely biological beings. Above all, if people think that religion can persecute people, the thought itself is a blasphemous act, and it is dreadful that science has put a sharp knife to be used as a tool of persecution in the hands of religion instead of trying to protect people from the unscientific practices of religion. I believe that true God saves even evil people as well as sinners without judging them, as evidenced by the behavior of Jesus Christ, who protected a woman caught in adultery from the attack by the mob. This is the reason why a new paradigm is required. In a new scientific paradigm, religion and science should stop meaningless conflicts between them in the future.

The reason we human beings have two genetic sexes, male and female, is to prevent the overcombination of germ cells. This is related to the fact that we humans are still essentially protists that form only two types of germ cells. Females (female gametophytes) come into being as a result of the coincidental growth of the fertilized egg that resulted from the combination of the sperm with the X sex chromosome with an egg, and females produce eggs. Between sperms and eggs, only eggs have the cytoplasm. The reason eggs have cytoplasm is to prevent the collision of the cytoplasm in fertilized eggs by germ cell differentiation and supply nutrients. Women with eggs can become pregnant because humans are descendants of mammals that evolved through the age of dinosaurs. Women cannot become pregnant alone, and this means that women may become pregnant regardless of their will or intent. All living things live according to the principle of the precedence of survival over reproduction, and women are responsible for pregnancy and childbirth even though their individual values for survival (self-realization) are infringed upon. This is the essential nature of feminism. Women's pregnancy and childbirth are self-sacrificing labor from the viewpoint of our species, Homo sapiens. Nevertheless, if women are punished for abortions that they have no choice but to undergo in order to prevent infringement on their values for survival, it is not scientifically appropriate. It is an uncivilized act that is in conflict with the spirit of the French Revolution, which is the starting point of modern democracy based on the principle that all humans are equal and the freedom of individuals should not be infringed upon without reasons. Only the relevant woman has the right to decide whether or not to give birth to a child, and this right should be properly respected in terms of all aspects, including social, medical, religious, and legal aspects. Therefore, from the perspective of new biology, we should not impose any restrictions on abortions.

The principle of the precedence of survival over reproduction applies to other organisms as well as humans. When food is scarce, South Africa's Cape fur seals abort their fetuses en masse, and thousands of baby seal carcasses are found floating around on the sea. For another example, a pregnant spotted eagle ray has an abortion when it is stressed. These examples show that the survival of the mother takes precedence over reproduction. The biological causes of menopause in women and adolescent infertility in primates can be explained in the same way. These phenomena occur because pregnancy and childbirth pose obstacles to the survival of mothers when mothers are too young or senile. In other words, it is a tactic for preventing pregnancy rather than having an abortion. In the same vein, all animals have a period during which sexual maturity occurs, as shown by the fact that teenage girls' periods start at a certain age. On the other hand, in the case of sand tiger sharks, females have two uteri and get 50 fertilized eggs to develop in each uterus. The first-hatched embryo in each uterus consumes all the siblings hatched later and unhatched eggs in the uterus and grows to about 1m in size when the mother gives birth to two offspring, one from each utero. This is a survival strategy of sand tiger sharks that allows them to survive without being eaten by fierce predators around their habitat. I claim that their strategy of sacrificing other embryos to breed a single viable baby with the greatest likelihood for survival is not in conflict with biological principles.

What is a biological explanation of sexual minorities? The fact that there are only two genetic sexes, female and male, has nothing to with evolutionary biological genders or social genders in each species of multicelluar organisms.

According to Lamarckism, all living organisms adapt to the environment as the agents of survival and reproduction in their respective ecological niches by 'an internal force.' Therefore, the occurrence of multiple genders and homosexuality in each animal species and human life is a result of adaptation in terms of evolutional biology. In other words, not two genetic sexes in Darwin's theory but social genders resulting from 'an internal force' mentioned in Lamarck's theory are true genders of each species. The males of a lizard species native to the Central Valley in California, U.S. have three types of genders. This is due to the fact that it is impossible for them to reproduce only with one gender because their habitat covers a very large area or shows large year-to-year changes in environmental conditions. The phenomenon of homosexuality of males or females or the appearance of multiple genders from males or females due to environmental factors is often observed not only among fish species but also among bird species or mammals (See '*Evolution's Rainbow*' by Joan Roughgarden).

Homosexuality is a biological phenomenon that occurs because men, who tend to have a freer way of thinking and bear greater responsibility for supporting the family than women, concentrated more on survival than reproduction in an extremely poor environment for survival during the industrial revolution. In this case, men's getting married and having and raising children correspond to reproductive behaviors, while their focusing on affection and experience with other men corresponds to acts for survival. Thus, homosexuality is a biological adaptation phenomenon. It is comparable to the adaptation of ants, in whose society the queen is entirely responsible for reproduction. Men tend to think more freely because women have less daily experience due to restrictions on their daily and social activities because of pregnancy and childbirth. There are no other reasons for differences in thinking between men and women. Men have a larger body and tend to be aggressive because they need to protect women and children and need to perform greater actions in the performance of sexual activity, and there are no other reasons for physical differences between men and women. All gender differences in traits are evolutionary results of use and disuse. Adaptation for survival occurs primarily in all the species of living organisms. Thus, women are never inferior to men in any adaptive traits for survival other than the above described traits of males. Especially in intelligence, there are no gender differences. I think that

Jesus Christ selected me, a woman, as an advocate of Christ in order to prove this point.

According to the above-mentioned book '*Evolution's Rainbow*', there are many examples of the presence of male-like females and female-like males in each animal species. Transgender people can be regarded as such a case. Since men and women live together in a human society, there may be men that are disposed toward a feminine personality and appearance and women that are disposed toward a masculine personality and appearance, and the results are shown in neurons and alleles. Because the genetic information of species that reproduce by sexual reproduction is randomly assigned to genetically diverse individuals through the formation and fertilization of germ cells, it is not possible to predict who will be born and grow with the sexual orientations of transgender persons. In all the species of animals, neurons are responsible for adaptation at the forefront of the environment. In other words, they are agents of genetic diversity for efficient adaptation of the members of each species, and at the same time, they are agents that implement the new methods of adaptation when large and small changes in the environment occur. Evolution occurs in each specific species along with the formation of a new ecological niche when there are large changes in environmental factors. In addition, the exploration of neurons in accordance with the principle of the precedence of survival over reproduction results in a genetic system, and this process is intended to automate the adaptation process to achieve maximally efficient adaptation.

The principle of the precedence of survival over reproduction is also corroborated by the forms of marriage in human societies. The extratribal marriage of primitive tribes was intended to prevent genetic deformities, and monogamy in civilized societies functions as the best possible method for preventing unnecessary conflicts over affection. Polygyny is adopted in societies where wealth is concentrated in the family due to environmental factors or the number of males is smaller due to the occurrence of a war or other factors. On the other hand, polyandry is carried out in extremely harsh environments such as Ladakh. These forms of marriage are all intended to ensure the survival of as many members of the society as possible. In other words, the form of marriage as a social institution is determined as the method that maximally guarantees the survival stability of the members of the society not only genetically but also socially in the environment where each ethnic group lives.

Now, I will describe the third reason for writing this letter. The world is now facing a very serious global crisis due to climate changes, and Christ ordered President Macron to perform a leading role in global endeavors to overcome this crisis because President Macron has the cosmic aspiration that he will benefit the whole world. Humans, the species Homo sapiens, are the animal species that reached the final stage of evolution, and since we humans adapt to the environment by using intelligence, we have conquered the entire Earth as the lord of all creation. After going through primitive times, we humans soon entered the age of civilization, and we are now enjoying unprecedented material abundance through the development of science and technology. However, our material abundance has been obtained at the cost of putting the Earth, our home, in a crisis situation due to global warming and endangering ourselves and biological diversity or all kinds of living organisms, which are our biological relatives that contributed to the existence of our species from an evolutionary perspective. How can we overcome this global crisis? Jesus Christ, who has become God, ordered us Home sapiens to believe in ourselves. What does it mean that we should believe in ourselves? How can we believe in ourselves?

If you don't mind, I would like to tell you a little more about myself. You may wonder what kind of person I am and how come I decided to write this letter to you. I ask you to take note of my scientific discoveries obtained through five years of arduous research and the bold method I used to make my findings known and accepted as a scientific theory. No matter how perspicacious and capable I am, could I have done all of these things without divine interventions? What do you think of this? Since I first got the impression thought that Darwinism is erroneous and Lamarckism is correct, I didn't expect to receive anyone's help except for God's help. I had never gone to church before I entered university, but as a college freshman, I had the chance to read the Bible due to the suggestion of an evangelical Christian student. On the day when I first read the Bible, Jesus appeared in front of me and said, "The truth will set you free." I thought that what Jesus told me was that 'truth exists not in a narrow world without God but in a wide world where God is present.' This realization immediately led me to believe in God. However, even after the experience, I did not live a life with strong religious passion as a devout Christian, and in my adulthood, I lived a miserable life due to long-term depression, marital conflicts, and my occupation that did not match my personality.

When I was on the brink of divorce, my previous clients in divorce proceedings strongly dissuaded me from getting divorced. To overcome a serious marital crisis, I started to study the personality psychology of married couples from the perspective of evolutional biology around 2010. As a result, I found that human beings evolved into people with two types of personality: the rational type and the emotional type. The rational people predominantly use the frontal lobe of the brain, while the emotional people predominantly use the amygdala of the brain. Through this research on personality, I arrived at the conclusion that individuals with opposite personalities get married to maximize their adaptability in monogamous societies. By applying this conclusion to myself and my husband as a married couple, I was able to overcome my marital conflicts almost immediately. I thought that humans can selectively make a predominant use of the frontal lobe and the amygdala and that people of the emotional type could overcome their depression if they predominantly use the frontal lobe. Actually, I succeeded in curing my depression immediately by applying this theory to myself. Subsequently, I shared my experience with people, but most people seemed to think that since I was an intelligent person, I managed to overcome my depression and marital problems in such a way. Therefore, to introduce my findings to more people and gain an opportunity for the objective evaluation of my findings, I decided to write a book. Then, while I was trying to write a book on the personality types of married couples, I encountered the evolutional theories of Darwinism and Lamarckism in 2017, as I described in the first page of this letter.

When I was a high school student, I heard the expression 'the person to consummate Western civilization' ringing in my ears countless times, and when I was young, I frequently muttered to myself, "I will become successful in life like the sun in the future." Last year, when I was reviewing 'conflicts between religion and science', which is a topic dealt with in the latter part of my book, I heard the voice of God saying, "I have been waiting for you. I am the science." Then, I finally realized that when I first met Jesus at the age of twenty, He gave me my true calling in life, which is to seek truth. At the end of last year, I was 'accepted as righteous by God' through a dream. This year, I also realized that God sent me as 'an advocate for Jesus' after training me as a lawyer, as Jesus promised to send an advocate as written in the Gospel of John. (I have always had a strong desire and great aspiration for success throughout my life, but I was not fully satisfied with anything until I happened to have an opportunity to challenge the truthfulness of Darwin's evolutionary theory. For this reason, I was able to empathically understand Jesus as the being that was born as a human being but came to embrace an unattainable wish to help humans by becoming God. Although this comparison may seem rather disrespectful to Jesus, I think that the impression I have made on my contemporaries is probably similar to the impression that the Jewish clergy had of Jesus about two thousand years ago in the days of Jesus.) This year, I have been unexpectedly appointed as the vice president of the Korean Bar Association, and this duty has given me an opportunity for me to reconcile myself with my job as a lawyer that I have not been in harmony with due to my personality. When I looked back on my past life, I realized that God has always been with me throughout my life. If I derive reconciliation between science and religion with President Macron's help, as an advocate of Jesus and as the daughter of Lamarck that has returned, will it lead to the consummation of Western civilization? The intrinsic nature of God is brilliance like the sun. If I stand as a lawyer for

Jesus before humanity, doesn't it mean that I have become a brilliantly successful person like the sun?

When Jesus left us two thousand years ago, he promised that he would return to us. I believe this promise since God always keeps His promises, He is returning this time, and my duty is to promulgate truth and thereby proclaim His coming back to us. I think that Jesus wants to eradicate not only the arrogance of intellectuals that deny the presence of God and worship Darwin like a god but also the ignorance of religious people that stick to old, obsolete knowledge that has been passed down from people that lived two thousand years ago. By nature, God feels delighted when human beings enjoy freedom in the light of truth (knowledge), and He gives comfort and peace to humans when they live in the darkness of ignorance (destiny). This is believed to be 'a new divine order' that will prevail not only in academic activities including scientific research but also in all the areas of human life in the future. When humans engage in thinking, a paradigm plays a very important role. A fallacious paradigm precludes true communication between people, so it inevitably gives rise to numerous and continuous conflicts. Since the Darwinian paradigm is the root cause of constant conflicts between religion and science as well as the continuous occurrence of religious, racial, and gender conflicts, God has come to judge people advocating such a paradigm. Moreover, Richard Dawkins, who may be considered an authentic successor of Charles Darwin, made a blasphemous remark that 'God is a delusion and a brain parasite.'

However, from the perspective of Lamarckism, God is the supreme scientific being, theism is recognized as a universal truth, it is no longer possible to question the existence of God and claim the absence of God even though people have freedom to believe in or not to believe in God. This is what I realized at the age of 20, when I thought that 'truth exists in the world where God is present,' In other words, God is always with us eternally, and this is believed to be the fulfillment of God's promise to give eternal life to us. In addition, God was always with me while I was finding out the flaws of Darwin's theory of evolution, This fact indicates that God approved Lamarck's theory of evolution, which allows us to take the perspective that all living things coexist peacefully. In the future, science will focus on proving the scientific nature (adaptability) of God and recognize Lamarckism as a universal theory of evolution. On the other hand, religion will not receive any kind of threat from science and focus on its intrinsic function of providing peace without judging or persecuting people. In this way, science and religion will have their respective unique areas that are distinct from each other, and they will cooperate with each other.

Why is God returning during our time? I think it is due to the fact that although humans have made remarkable advancements in science and technology with the change of the times over time, science and religion have been antagonistic towards each other by using fallacious and outdated knowledge as their weapons, and conflicts between science and religion have now worsened to an unacceptable degree. According to Lamarckism, religious, racial, international, and gender conflicts can be easily resolved. All phenomena are results of adaptation of each species or the members of each species to the given environment, so relationships based on superiority and inferiority or competitive relationships between different species or individuals cannot be established. In addition, active adaptations of each species or their members can occur anew at any time, depending on the circumstances. For example, gender conflicts can be resolved by establishing policies that prevent women's pregnancy, childbirth, or child rearing from obstructing women's adaptation for survival. These days, feminineness and masculinity are manifested by the appearances of males and females and the way a man and a woman love each other. These feminineness and masculinity are very beautiful, so I think that feminineness and masculinity should be regarded as the realm of individual freedom and they should be allowed and accepted as the way they are. I also think that we can avoid unnecessary conflicts by overcoming feminism as an ideology. Moreover, in the midst of an unprecedented global crisis due to climate changes, people feel confused and agitated. At this moment, an armed conflict is happening in Ukraine, and many people have become involved in the war against their will. Therefore, we now need peace, solace, and tranquility from God more than ever.

Now, I would like to explain why God chose President Macron and France. As described earlier, France is the country promoting the spirit of the French Revolution, such as liberty, equality, and fraternity. It is also the country of Jeanne d'Arc and Charles VII and the native country of Jean-Baptiste Lamarck and Ernest Renan. Furthermore, it is the country of a number of revolutions, including the revolution led by President Macron, and the French people have their own esprit and do not hesitate to realize truth. If we can achieve a revolution that can get rid of fallacious and outdated knowledge and achieve a new paradigm shift at once, do you think that such a revolution can occur in a country other than France on the Earth? I think that since God loves truth, He also loves people who love truth. Two thousand years ago, Pontius Pilate killed a being that would become God. I hope that President Macron will leave his name eternally as a great politician that gives great honor and glory to Jesus, the being that has become God and is coming back to us to proclaim the justice of God(Lamarckism), judge our sins(Darwinism) and give eternal life to humans(Presence of God).

The most mysterious aspect of a species is the harmonious co-adaptation of all the members, including males and females. We Homo sapiens will be able to overcome the climate crisis if the people all over the world, including a number of politicians, work together through President Macron's leading role, based on Lamarckism and the spirit of the French Revolution. According to Lamarckism, all species will cope actively with environmental changes, and the spirit of the French Revolution is that we will not only benefit all humanity on the planet and but also never tolerate defeat. Especially, the Lord is expecting us to make efforts to overcome this crisis by believing in our ability to wisely get through this crisis because humans as Homo sapiens are beings seeking continuous growth and improvement, as shown by the new paradigm shift that has occurred in our time. This is the message that Jesus Christ is sending to President Macron through me, and people around the world will hear the news from President Macron. Finally, I hope that we will open the great era of Homo sapiens through God's great blessing. I wish President Macron, Ambassador Philippe Lefort, and their families as well as all French people and all the people around the world good health and happiness. Thank you.

## Attachments

1. A copy of the book 'The Evolution of Sex through the Inheritance of Life History and Speciation as a result of the Use and Disuse of Organs'

2. A short introduction to and a book review of the above book with an English translation of each of them

3. A copy of the 2021 December issue of PowerKorea, a magazine published in Korea

4. A copy of a letter dated December 12, 2022 concerning

the scientific discovery report (and the request for the evaluation of scientific validity of the discovery) with an English translation of the letter

**Postscript**

I think President Macron and Ambassador Philippe Lefort may wonder why I am trying to bring biological problems to French politicians rather than Korean politicians or scientists even though I'm Korean. Thus, I would like to give some explanation about this question again. After I finished writing my book at the end of August last year, I sent the news about the publication of my book to several magazines in Korea, but this attempt failed to elicit any particular attention to my findings from Korean science magazines or scientists. Despite the overall indifference toward my findings, I sent the scientific discovery report (the fourth attachment among the attachments listed above) on December 22, 2021 in an attempt to dedicate our gift to Jesus on Christmas for the first time in human history, and this effort also proved fruitless. On January 5, 2022, I accidentally learned that a trial on the abortion rights of American women was pending in the U.S. Supreme Court. Upon hearing the news, I wanted to help those fighting for abortion rights, so I sent the letter about my findings to about ten eminent scientists, a reporter of Time newspaper, the HBES Annual Conference (application for participation), and the Guttmacher Institute, an organization advocating women's abortion rights in the U.S. The HBES notified me of the rejection of my application, and other individuals or organizations did not even give any reply to me. Regarding my trustworthiness as a person, if you ask the executives and staff of the Korean Bar Association about my character, they will confirm my integrity and trustworthiness because I have been working with them since I was appointed as the vice president this year. I have enclosed the business card in case you want to ask the president of the Korean Bar Association about me.

Finally, I would like to reemphasize the significance of my scientific findings regarding the evolution of sex and the new speciation. My biological findings are a very important event related to the fulfillment of numerous prophesies, including the prediction made by the Chinese philosopher Lao Tzu in B.C. 600, the promise of the Second Coming of Jesus Christ, Lamarck's daughter's prediction, Charles Darwin's prediction, and the voice prophesy about the person to consummate Western civilization that I heard as a high

school student. Thus, I sincerely implore President Macron and Ambassador Philippe Lefort not to dismiss this letter as not worth considering. Do you know about Baba Vanga's prophecies for the year 2021? Baba Vanga was a Bulgarian clairvoyant called the Nostradamus of the Balkans, and she predicted that a powerful dragon would seize humanity in 2021. The moment I heard the prophecy, I realized that the dragon referred to me. On May 12, 2021, I also wrote the following declaration on my Facebook page: "I will shatter Darwinism into stone dust." Five days later, on May 17, I heard the news about the collapse of Darwin's Arch, which is situated to the southeast of Darwin Island in the Galápagos Archipelago. I thought that this incident symbolized the end of Charles Darwin's evolutionary theory.
Thank you.

Sincerely yours,


Sung Hee Kwon
(A South Korean lawyer, Vice president of the Korean Bar Association)

September 29, 2022

## The woman lawyer who hears God's Voice declares Christ's Second Coming for American women whose abortion rights have been violated

PowerKorea met Kwon Sung-hee, who recently published a Korean-English book
<Can Macron offer Biden the Restoration of Women's Abortion Rights?>

Does God need lawyers? Jesus Christ, who came to this earth 2,000 years ago, seemed to think it was necessary. Around the world, atheism has long been rampant among intellectuals, including scientists, and God has been mocked. Not only this. Believers in God have forgotten their religious duties and are taking the lead in persecuting people. To make it clear, neither is God's true form. So God has decided to come again, just as He had promised long ago. But before that, He has sent a lawyer as his representative to deliver the news.

Then, a person appeared who claimed to be this lawyer. August 2021, she published <The Evolution Of Sex Through The Inheritance Of Life History And Speciation As A Result Of

The Use And Disuse Of Organs>. It is a book that reveals the mechanism of sexual evolution and the validity of Lamarck's theory of evolution. Now her second book <Can Macron offer Biden the Restoration of Women's Abortion Rights?> (Feb 24, 2023 / Evolution and Humans) has been released, the woman lawyer Kwon Sung-hee who hears God's Voice delivers the message alongside her arguments on our special section. Below is the summary of the interview with her.

**Q1. So you say that Jesus Christ sends us a lawyer as His representative?**

Looking back, it was none other than an invitation from God, that I wrote my first book after fierce wandering of studying biology for 5 years from the strong impression that Darwin's theory of evolution was wrong. Chapters 14-16 of John's Gospel repeat Jesus' words to his disciples before his death that he would send the Advocate as his representative. Jesus also called it "the Holy Spirit," and later generations interpreted it as "the Holy Spirit, the Comforter."

The role given by Jesus to the advocate is to "praise and exalt Jesus by emphasizing his identity and teachings," "to define and enforce divine justice, sin, and judgment," and "to lead the world to all truth and to declare what is to come." So, after all, the advocate must be a person. I came across this verse while reading an English Bible at the end of last year, and as soon as I saw it, I was convinced it was me.

## Q2. How could you be sure that Jesus' representative lawyer was you?

Throughout my high school years, I heard the phrase in my mind many times that I was the one who consummate Western civilization. When I was a freshman in college, I was in the process of converting to Christianity, and as I was cleaning my hair in the basement washroom, Jesus was in front of me and said, "The truth will set you free." When I was in my late 40's, I heard Jehovah God's voice say: "Humans must stop being arrogant."

When I was in my 30s, I was pessimistic because I didn't have the aptitude to be a lawyer. Then I heard Jesus' voice saying, "You wanted it (the lawyer's job)." Looking back, I prayed a vow, saying, "If you pass me the bar exam, I will be better in believing in God." In fact, after graduating from high school, I couldn't think of studying in Seoul due to my family's circumstances. But Jesus also granted my wish to go to Seoul, and I made myself a judicial scholarship student at Ewha Women's University.

Last year, I was even honored to be the vice president of the Korean Bar Association. I thought that I was not qualified to be a vice president because I neglected my lawyer's job for the last 4~5 years due to writing a book. But come to think of it, this book wouldn't have come out if I hadn't joined the Korean Bar Association.

**Q3. Scientists and intellectuals around the world take the stand of atheists. So for them, what you're saying can be hard to believe. How do you think?**

I perused 400 biology books. This confirms the scientific validity of Lamarck's theory of evolution. And if I hadn't written a book revealing this, I would have thought the same like them (scientist and intellectuals). I came to believe in God through Jesus' direct evangelism, but I failed to become an institutional Christian. I think the reason was that I didn't know enough about God's science.

God is a scientific being that evolved along with Homo sapiens, who acquired language as a tool for thinking in the process of evolution of the genus Homo and lived by knowledge, while coping with the ignorance that constantly causes anxiety. In Lamarck's theory of evolution, God and man are twins. So it's no wonder I hear God's voice.

**Q4. According to a theory of evolution, you say Gods exist or not exist? We are confused.**

This is a time when science is very advanced, and people think within the scientific paradigm. In his book <The Structure of Scientific Revolutions>, eminent historian of science Thomas Kuhn said that 'recognizing functional deficiencies that cause crises in both political and scientific development is a prerequisite for revolution.'

Darwin's theory of evolution sees life as a machine for genes to replicate themselves. This means that it could not explain the 'scientificity of women's abortions and the sexual minorities that do not accompany childbirth (reproduction)'.

Scientism pushes everything that cannot be measured 'as unscientific', so it blasphemes God as a delusion or the parasite in the brain. But according to Lamarck evolution, these are all very typical life phenomena.

Darwin's theory of evolution has no role either scientifically or politically and therefore should be discarded.

**Q5. You say a paradigm shift. Does this mean that in Lamarckism, God, abortion, and sexual minorities are scientific phenomena?**

The perfect God is a scientific companion who evolved to be with imperfect humans. God is the one who wipes away tears when women conceive an unwelcome child and people struggle with their identity or when they are in such pain. Just because human beings can distinguish good from evil through language as an excellent thinking tool does not immediately make them a god-like being. The biological meaning of "original sin" is that humans are merely "animals that can speak." God does not judge, acknowledging that this is a human condition.

Jesus Christ fits the Lamarckian view of God in every way. "I have not come to judge the world, but to save," and "Sinners and the sick need me." as Jesus said. God is a being who stays with humans forever unless they become extinct. Most of Christ's words, such as "You did not choose me, but I chose you" and "I will be with you until the end of the world" fit the scientific facts very well.

**Q6. The scientific community has long been dominated by Darwinism, so how is the transition to Lamarckism possible?**

Evolution is the principle by which male and female members of a species are formed. The evolution of sex in biology is unknown. As I explained in detail in a book published two years ago, when I discovered the mechanism of sex evolution, it was impossible to discuss speciation without knowing the evolution of sex. That's why the existing biological community unreasonably sided with Darwin.

Organisms are divided into prokaryotes, eukaryotic unicellular organisms (let's call them "protists" for convenience) and multicellular organisms. Protists and multicellular organisms inherit the life history and traits of prokaryotes, their progenitors. And they evolved sexual reproduction in the process of modifying and adapting it to suit the presence or absence of a nucleus and multicellularity.

It is the official position of the scientific community that, Endosymbiotic theory, eukaryotic single-celled organisms evolved through predation events among prokaryotes. Plants as well as animals in the early stages of evolution live a fixed life in water. So I deduced that protists acquired multicellularity through underwater sedimentation and evolved into multicellular organisms. If so, it must be said that all living things have prokaryotic properties. Therefore, it appears that prokaryotic life history or traits are also expressed in descendants as needed.

**Q7. Please enlighten us with the details of Lamarck's theory of evolution.**

There is only one law that governs all living things: the pre-survival, post-reproduction. All living things first consolidate their survival and then reproduce. All living things in the three realms form ecological status, which means that they will coexist peacefully by eliminating competition that is dangerous to their survival. Sexual reproduction, which evolved in the process of protists seeking survival when the environment is unfavorable and then reproducing after the environment improves, is also a phenomenon of pre-survival, post-reproduction.

In the case of sexual reproduction of multicellular organisms, the queen reproduction, sex change, monogamy, polygamy, and sexual dimorphism are also the result of presurvival, post-reproduction. Multicellular organisms act in an ecological niche by first securing survival and then reproducing.

Therefore, the Lamarck's core theory of evolution, 'simultaneous evolution of male and female by the use and disuse of organs' and my 'pre-survival post-reproduction' inevitably go hand in hand. Each species of multicellular organisms is evolved when the male and female acquire the survival traits jointly first, and then acquire the reproductive traits separately but simultaneously.

**Q8. Does this mean that the origin of sex and male and female formation has been clarified?**

The reason multicellular organisms are male and female is derived from that when protists reproduce sexually, they form only two germ cells: sperm and egg. This is to prevent over-splicing, and excessive number of chromosomes results in malformations and infertility. Multicellular organisms that evolved by acquiring multicellularity from protists, also form only sperm and eggs. Protists are sexless because they form two gametes from the somatic cell. Even in multicellular organisms, descendant organisms that evolved earlier form sperm and egg as hermaphrodites.

However, since animals live while moving, it is not easy to crossfertilize as a hermaphrodite body. From echinoderms and mollusks with much movement, male and female gametophytes are separated (male and female bodies) but evolve simultaneously, producing each eggs and sperm at the same time and reproducing by sexual intercourse. This is the origin of sex.

## Q9. What does it mean to distinguish between biological and social gender?

The biological sex of multicellular organisms is male and female derives from the formation of only two germ cells from protists: sperm and egg. However, each species of living beings additionally adapts in its respective ecological status, so social sex (gender) appears, and this is the true sex of that species.

Bees and ants, clownfish and naked mole rats reproduce only in queens. The reason is that, in their ecological status, if all females reproduce, the members of that species do not have a single chance of survival. They are divided into two genders: the breeding queen and the infertile female. Clownfish are divided into two male genders: one breeding male per queen and several immature males, but there is no problem with the biological adaptation of all these individuals.

This means that all living things are the first to survive, and reproduction is not a problem even if they don't do it according to the situation. It's awkward to compare humans to insects and fish, but I think we can understand that the same biological paradigm applies to our LGBTI phenomenon. After all, we humans are living things.

**Q10. The book's subtitle is 'Lamarck has returned with Jesus Christ'. You proudly claim the Second Coming of Christ. But do you think that makes sense?**

According to the Gospel of John, the authority that Jesus granted to the lawyer is limited to "(the agent) does not speak according to his own thoughts, but as he has received and heard (from Jesus)." However, it is comprehensive, defining God's justice, sin, and judgment, proclaiming all truth, and declaring what is to come.

The term here should be taken to mean within the Lamarckism paradigm. After all, it must be said that Lamarckism is God's justice and Darwinism is God's sin, judgment is done accordingly, and this is all truth.

In the Bible, signs of Jesus' Second Coming are detailed in Mark (chapter 13), Matthew (chapter 24), and Luke (chapter 21). One of them, "people being persecuted because of Jesus," would include the intellectuals and scientists today who claim atheism as if it were science and despise those who believe in God.

I cautiously speculate that 'I see an abomination standing in a holy place' means that the temple is being used as a different place. There are also signs that 'great tribulation will come that has never been and will never come that day' and that 'women who are pregnant and those who have nursing babies on that day are dreadful.' Is it unreasonable to interpret it as 'women who are pregnant and with nursing babies suffer horribly because of the violation of abortion rights in the United States today' if I judge from the fact that Jesus' words, "I will rebuild the destroyed temple in three days," were interpreted by the disciples as being resurrected in three days?

Isn't the phrase 'lightning flashes from the east and flashes to the west' a metaphor for my involvement as an Asian? Jesus promised: "I will not leave you orphans, but I will return." I believe that God always keeps His promises. Jesus is coming to judge intellectuals and scientists for taking God from people and turning them into orphans, and for religious people to persecute aborted women and sexual minorities.

## Q11. Why did President Macron and President Biden appear in the title of the book?

Biden is the president of the Democratic Party of the United States and is working to reclaim women's abortion rights. President Macron expressed solidarity with American women as president of the homeland of Lamarck, the founder of biology. If the two presidents knew my scientific findings, they wouldn't stand idly by for American women, so I put them in the title of the book.

Modern democracies would be blessed to have wise leaders like them. May my discovery be widely publicized so that, as the Bible promises, 'the day may be shortened for those whom God chose.' I wish President Biden a smooth re-election.

**Q12. If what you said above were to be known in the religious, scientific, and political worlds, the impact would be enormous.**

The key is that my findings must be known and their scientific justification recognized. If the scientific nature of sexual evolution and the new theory of evolution are recognized, then the Second Coming of Christ should be recognized accordingly. When I finished the book in August 2021, I thought, "I am in charge of the Second Coming of Jesus and of consummating Western civilization through integration of religion and science." From then on I called myself 'Latter-day John the Baptist,' and by the guidance of Christ's voice, I have come to the present.

Christ encourages us to pursue the truth in earnest, believing in the potential of "us, talking animals." Truth is not only our right, but also our duty.

www.ingramcontent.com/pod-product-compliance
Lightning Source LLC
Chambersburg PA
CBHW040221170726
48295CB00014B/761